ACC. No: 07056257

Also by Nick Ward

The Charlie Small Journals
Gorilla City
Pirate Galleon
Destiny Mountain
The Puppet Master's Prison
The Underworld
Frostbite Pass
The Mummy's Tomb
Forest of Skulls
Planet of the Gerks
Land of the Remotosaurs
The Hawk's Nest
The Final Showdown

Alfie Small
Serpents and Scarecrows
Ug and the Dinosaurs
Captain Thunderbolt and the Jelloids
Pirates and Dragons

Superbot
Superbot and the Terrible Toy Destroyer
Superbot: Toad and the Goo Extractor

The Night's Realm

Nick Ward

David Fickling Books

31 Beaumont Street
Oxford OX1 2NP, UK

The Night's Realm
is a
DAVID FICKLING BOOK

First published in Great Britain in 2019 by
David Fickling Books
31 Beaumont Street,
Oxford, OX1 2NP

Text and illustrations © Nick Ward, 2019

978-1-78845-043-0

1 3 5 7 9 10 8 6 4 2

The right of Nick Ward to be identified as the author and illustrator of this work has been asserted in accordance with the Copyright, Designs and Patents Act 1988.

All rights reserved. No part of this publication may be reproduced, stored in a retrieval system, or transmitted in any form or by any means, electronic, mechanical, photocopying, recording or otherwise, without the prior permission of the publishers.

Papers used by David Fickling Books are from well-managed forests and other responsible sources.

DAVID FICKLING BOOKS Reg. No. 8340307

A CIP catalogue record for this book is available from the British Library.

Typeset in 12/19 pt Sabon by Falcon Oast Graphic Art Ltd.
Printed and bound in Clays Ltd, Elcograf S.p.A

Permission: From *Cider with Rosie* by Laurie Lee. Published by *Chatto and Windus*. Reprinted by permission of Random House Group Limited © 1959

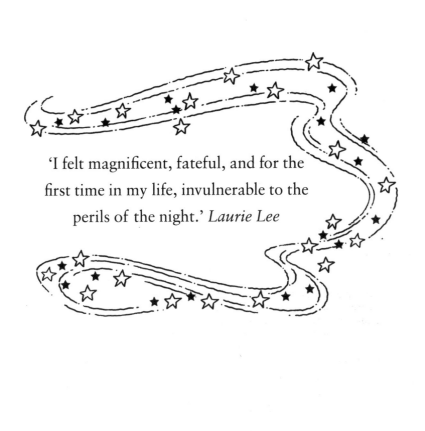

'I felt magnificent, fateful, and for the first time in my life, invulnerable to the perils of the night.' *Laurie Lee*

'Are you scared of the dark? Well, you should be. You may think you are immune to the terrors of the night, but you are not. Nobody is.

I am the Magician, ruler of the Night's Realm, and my dark fortress stretches as far as the eye can see. I have hundreds of children working for me, but I need more. Their fear is my lifeblood – it gives me my power.

One of my trusted warlocks tells me there are lots more children ready for the taking. Are you one of them? Soon, when the night is at its darkest, I may come for you. And once I have you here, I will keep you for ever.

1

Billy Jones was crossing the park on his way home from school, kicking an old tennis ball about with his friend Tom.

'No way!' he said, hoofing the ball into the air. 'Really?'

'Yep,' said Tom, heading it back to Billy.

Saturday was Tom's birthday, and he was getting an X-Station from his mum and dad.

'So, d-do you f-fancy coming over to my place?' he asked, stammering slightly as he always did.

'Definitely,' said Billy, catching the ball and putting it in his pocket. 'I'm not going to miss out on an all-day gaming session.'

They made their way out through the park gates and up the hill to a row of small shops.

'Hold on a bit,' said Billy, stopping outside the convenience store on the corner and feeling in his pockets for some change.

He pushed the door open and immediately headed to the sweets. He grabbed a bag of his favourites and took them to the checkout. Mrs Rutland was usually behind the till, but today a crooked elderly man was standing there instead. He was an odd-looking person and Billy had to force himself not to stare. The man's long nose and curved chin almost touched at their ends, and he was as bald as a coot and as wrinkled as a dried prune. If he believed in such things, Billy might have mistaken him for some sort of evil wizard or warlock.

'Hi! Where's Mrs Rutland?' asked Billy,

trying to stop himself from wrinkling his nose. The man gave off a strong, musty odour.

'She's not well, I'm afraid,' said the man. He breathed noisily through his open mouth and sounded like a blocked drain. He scrutinized Billy intently. 'I'll be standing in for her until she's better.'

Tom appeared beside Billy with a can of Coke and waited as the strange man scanned Billy's sweets.

'That'll be one pound twenty,' the man said, but as Billy went to take the bag, the man held onto it and wouldn't let go. He stared at Billy with eyes as dark as a bottomless well. It seemed to go on for ages, and an icy shudder ran down Billy's spine.

Then with a knowing smile, the man let go and Billy paid, snatched the bag up and hurried outside. He felt a slight stinging on his wrist, and saw he'd scratched himself. There was a little red mark, shaped like a tick. Billy felt thoroughly unsettled, and took a few deep breaths to calm down.

Tom followed a few seconds later. 'W-w-what was all that about?' he asked, popping open his can and taking great gulps of Coke.

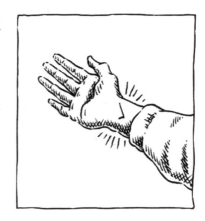

'No idea,' said Billy, starting to feel better now he was out in the sunshine. 'He was really creepy, though!'

Tom frowned and glanced at his own wrist. 'I've been scratched,' he said, licking the wound.

'Me too,' said Billy. 'I think it was that old man's fingernails. They were like claws.'

'Maybe,' said Tom, draining his drink and lobbing the can into a nearby bin. 'Anyway, about this Saturday – could you c-c-come over for half ten?'

'Sure,' said Billy.

'Brilliant,' said Tom. 'And m-m-my mum said you could stay over, so we can play all night too if we're quiet!'

'You mean stay the night?' asked Billy, his chest feeling suddenly tight.

'Yeah. What's the p-problem?'

'I can't,' said Billy. His skin started to prickle and his heart began to race. 'I – er – I've just remembered my cousins are visiting this weekend, and I've got to stay and keep them company.'

'You're j-joking, aren't you?' said Tom.

'Sorry,' said Billy, shrugging apologetically but feeling a huge wave of relief. 'Perhaps I can come another time.'

'Whatever,' said Tom, with a disappointed sigh. 'I'll see you at s-s-school tomorrow.'

'Sorry,' said Billy again, as they parted company to go their different ways home. He wandered past the cinema and up into Merlin Place, his face burning with shame. He hated lying to his best mate just to wriggle out of a situation he couldn't cope with, but he didn't want to become a laughing stock either.

For the fact was, Billy Jones was afraid of the dark.

* * *

Billy had been scared of the dark for as long as he could remember, but lately his fear had become much worse. He'd started seeing things lurking in the shadows of his room – creeping, crawling things that made his muscles freeze in terror and the breath judder in his chest. It made him feel stupid and ashamed. It was why he now kept a night light on in his bedroom, and why he couldn't have stayed over at Tom's house.

'Hi, Mum!' Billy called, as he clattered through the front door and dumped his bag in the hall.

'Good day at school?' asked his mum, as usual.

'Oh, wonderful!' said Billy sarcastically. He didn't mention Tom's birthday – she would only try and persuade him to go. Although they knew he had a problem with the dark, his mum and dad weren't aware how bad it had become.

Billy tried not to think about the approaching night, but as he played computer games up in his bedroom the sky outside began to darken, sending shadows stretching and creeping through the streets of the town. The evening seemed to fly by, and all too soon his dad called upstairs with the words he dreaded most.

'Time for bed, Billy.'

'OK,' croaked Billy, his voice a little shaky from a sense of looming peril. It was the same every evening. As soon as bedtime approached, all of his fears started to bubble up inside him. He tried to put it off for as long as possible, but after he'd been called twice and warned once, Billy got ready and went downstairs. His mum and dad were sat on the settee, watching TV.

'Night,' said Billy.

'Goodnight, sleep tight.'

Billy hung around in the doorway. His heart started to thump as he desperately tried to think of ways to delay the inevitable climb back upstairs.

'Off you go, Billy,' said his dad. 'You've got school in the morning.'

'OK,' he murmured in a small voice. He gave them each a peck on the cheek and then slowly went up to his room. He felt alone and helpless, and checked beneath his bed to make sure his torch and cricket bat were to hand. Then he climbed under the duvet, hoping beyond hope he wouldn't get another panic attack in the night. He read until he couldn't keep his eyes open any more, and finally drifted into a restless sleep.

2

Thump! A loud noise at Billy's window had him sitting bolt upright, his eyes staring and heart pounding. It was the dead of the night and he could see the silhouette of a figure crouched outside on his windowsill! It moved across the curtains, casting shadows on his bedroom wall. Billy rubbed at his sleep-filled eyes, and when he looked back the figure had gone.

He sighed with relief – but now the shadows in his room deepened and stretched, and the walls appeared to close in around him. He could hear a soft, menacing hissing, as if a

huge python was close by. The air turned cold and Billy's heart began to pound. He felt his duvet move, and something clammy grabbed his ankle.

'Get off!' he screamed, kicking out with his other foot and striking something hard. There was a hiss of frustration and a dark shape scuttled across the floor. It disappeared into the deep shadows in the corner of the room.

'Dad!' Billy yelled. 'Help!'

He turned on his bedside light, just as his dad came hurrying in.

'What's wrong?' his dad asked dopily, still half-asleep.

'Something in my room,' panted Billy, pointing to the corner. 'It grabbed me. Tried to pull me out of bed.'

'Oh, Billy,' sighed his dad. He went over to the corner, lifted a cardboard box of old toys out of the way and peered down the side of the wardrobe. 'Do you mean a rat or something?' he asked, grabbing a coat hanger and tentatively poking about.

'No, bigger than that,' said Billy.

'There's nothing here, Billy, nothing at all. Come and look.'

Billy climbed warily out of bed and edged towards the corner of his room. His dad was right.

'You were having a nightmare, that's all,' said Dad. 'OK?'

'OK,' said Billy, feeling confused and a little embarrassed for having caused such a fuss.

His mum came into the room, hair in a tangle and carrying a mug of warm cocoa. 'There's nothing to be frightened of, Billy,' she said, sitting on the edge of his bed. 'Come and drink this, it'll calm you down.'

Billy got back into bed and took the mug.

'What an imagination you have,' said his mum, with a smile.

Billy nodded, none too sure. He glanced

at the window. Of course there was nothing there. Had he been asleep or awake? It was hard to tell – with his mum and dad in the room everything seemed perfectly normal. But the figure on the sill had looked scarily real.

With a sigh Billy finished the drink and lay back on his pillow.

'Feeling better now?' asked Mum, straightening his duvet and giving him a kiss on the cheek.

Billy nodded.

'Good. Snuggle down and get some sleep or you'll be too tired for school in the morning.' She turned off the light and shuffled back to bed, but Billy's dad hovered in the doorway.

'I've got something for you,' he whispered mysteriously once she was gone, and disappeared into the spare room. Billy could hear him rummaging about in a cupboard. When he came back he was holding something in his hand. 'This might help,' he said with a smile of encouragement, and handed Billy something flat and round.

'It's a clock!' said Billy.

'A pocket watch,' said Dad.

Billy held it up and turned it round, so it caught the light. The watch had a white face with large numbers covered by a shiny dome of glass. In the middle, a semi-circular window showed an enamelled night sky. The back was engraved with the picture of a sword and a bronze sun, and it looked ancient – much older than the rest of the watch. It had a small button on one side. Billy pressed it and the back popped off.

Inside it was very plain, just a cover plate with a series of screws, but the reverse of the watch's back was as elaborately engraved as the outside, and showed the sun on a heraldic shield.

'Wow! It's awesome,' said Billy, clipping the back on again. It felt smooth and good to hold, but he wasn't sure why his dad had given it to him.

'It's a talisman – a sort of good-luck charm,' said Dad. 'Your grandad was given it when he went travelling as a young man.'

'Given it?' Billy asked, wondering who would give away such a wonderful thing.

'Well, he bought it, actually,' said Dad. 'From a wizened old mystic selling trinkets in an eastern bazaar. He said the sword was the symbol of an ancient order of knights, and that anyone who owned it would be protected.'

'Yeah, right. I bet he was just a con artist with a sack full of identical watches,' said Billy with a grin.

'That's what I thought,' said Dad. 'But your grandad insisted it helped him through a very dark time.'

'What sort of dark time?' asked Billy, intrigued.

'He wouldn't say,' said Dad, staring into space as he recalled things from a long time ago. 'He passed the watch on to me when I was having trouble with bullies at school.'

'I didn't know you were bullied,' said Billy in surprise.

'It's not something I like to talk about,' said Dad. 'But it was pretty serious stuff.'

'Did it work – did the watch protect you?'

'You bet,' said Dad, with a satisfied grin on his face.

Billy was itching to know more, but just then his mum called from the next room, 'Come on, Ted. Let Billy get some sleep. He's got school in the morning.'

'I'd better go!' said Dad.

Billy didn't know whether his dad had made the whole story up, just to make him feel better, but the watch was really cool so he put it on his bedside table and settled back under his duvet.

'Thanks, Dad,' he said. 'Night.'

'Goodnight, Billy,' said Dad, and tousled Billy's hair. 'Just remember, we're all frightened of something, but no fear is too big to overcome.'

'Goodnight,' mumbled Billy, as his dad turned off the light and went back to bed himself.

Billy turned on his side and closed his eyes, but try as he might he couldn't get back to sleep. His brain was too busy thinking. If he'd dreamed up the creature in his room, how come he could still feel where he'd been grabbed? He pulled up his pyjama leg and held his foot in the glow of his night light. There was a definite reddening of the skin where he'd been gripped.

'Knew it,' said Billy to himself. Then a frantic barking outside had him out of bed and scurrying across to the window.

He pulled back the corner of his curtain and looked out into the night. The narrow road was lit by pale orange street lamps and appeared deserted. Across the way in Mr Taylor's builder's yard though, his guard dog, Janus, was kicking up a stink, barking and scratching at the gap between the tall gates.

From the corner of his eye, almost invisible in the soft shadows, Billy saw a movement. Was it the silhouette of a figure? It was difficult to make out . . .

Easier to see was the pale, wild-haired creature at its feet! It was larger than a child,

but smaller than a full-grown man, and the sight of it made the hairs on the back of Billy's neck stand up. It was a creature straight out of his nightmares, and of all the things that haunted his dark dreams it was these creeping, crawling things that terrified him the most.

'That's it! That's what grabbed me,' gasped Billy, his heart thumping wildly as the shapes silently disappeared into the alley that ran between the houses. The moment they had gone, Janus stopped barking.

Still jittery, Billy climbed back into bed. He didn't know what to think. He couldn't talk to anybody about his fears. His mates would just take the mickey. Billy being scared of the dark at his age – what a wuss! And every time he had a nightmare, his parents said it was just his imagination, or asked if he was worried about something at school. But it was none of that. What he saw was real, he was sure it was.

Billy reached out from under the covers and took Grandad's pocket watch from his bedside table. It felt good in the palm of his hand, like a smooth, round pebble. He screwed his eyes tight shut and hoped his dad was right and that it would protect him from the terrors of the night.

3

Billy had become good at pushing any worries to the back of his mind, but his fear-filled night had seemed so real he was still jittery at school the following morning. At break time, as they sat on a low wall swapping Robo-warrior trading cards, Tom tried to convince him to stay over on his birthday once again.

'Go on, it'll be great. We'll be able to p-p-play all night!' said Tom, but Billy wasn't about to have a change of heart.

'Sorry, I just can't,' he said, feeling nauseous with worry and rubbing the tick-like scratch on his wrist that had begun to sting again. Then the bell went and they ambled in for afternoon lessons.

Tom was quiet all afternoon, and on the way home Billy could sense he was still disappointed.

'I tell you what,' he said. 'I could come over during the day. Mum says my cousins probably won't arrive till teatime.'

'Really? Excellent!' said Tom, brightening up immediately. 'Come as early as you can. I'm getting the latest F1 game, and I b-b-bet I'll beat you every time.'

'No chance,' laughed Billy, glancing into the convenience store as they passed by. He was glad to see that Mrs Rutland was back at work, and she gave him a cheery wave.

'See you tomorrow, then,' Billy said as he turned into Merlin Place and Tom carried on along Park Street. He checked his new pocket watch. It was four thirty and the little window in its face was now showing a radiant sun in a blue sky. Good, there was time for a computer game before tea.

He hurried up the drive, but before he reached the front door he heard a loud tapping noise. He was shocked to see a bird was trapped inside their front room. It was frantically pecking at the pane, trying to get out. It was a large bird – a jackdaw, Billy thought, and it was obviously distressed.

Whack! Billy jumped as the jackdaw hit the pane, leaving a smear of blood on the glass,

its beady eye wide with terror.

'Calm down,' he cried, sure the poor thing would kill itself if it didn't get out soon. He opened the front door and hurried inside.

'Mum, there's a bird in the house,' he called, dropping his school bag on the floor and going into the kitchen. But his mum wasn't there. 'Mum!' he yelled up the stairs, but there was still no reply. Perhaps she had popped to the shops.

Billy searched his bag for his mobile, to see if his mum had sent him a text – but now he could hear the jackdaw crashing around the front room and flailing against the door. He had to get the bird out, before it hurt itself. He turned the handle and flung the door open. The jackdaw came hurtling across the room towards him, its sharp beak open in a strident shriek. *'Carck!'*

'Get off!' Billy cried, and staggered backwards into the hall, fending off the jackdaw as it flapped and clawed at his face. He fumbled for the front door, tugged it open and rushed outside. As the bird flew off with a cackling laugh, Billy opened his eyes, and froze. A wave of fear surged through his body and his knees turned to jelly – for he had stepped out of the house and into the dark!

* * *

Billy couldn't believe his eyes. He was still on the street where he lived – there was Mr Taylor's house, and over there the builder's truck parked on the verge as always. But a moment before everything had been bathed in sunshine, and now it was all in darkness. Apart from the sound of the wind in the shrubs, everything was deadly quiet. What had happened – was it some sort of eclipse? With a trembling hand he checked his pocket watch. It still said four thirty, but now the little window was showing the night scene.

A knot of fear rose in his throat, bursting from his mouth as a terrified yell.

'HEEEELP! Is there anybody there? MUM, DAD. Please, somebody, HELP!'

Silence. There was no answering voice, no light came on in a window, and no dog barked in response.

His street was on a steep hill, and Billy could just make out the rest of the town from the glow of a weak moon. Everything looked the same, but not a single street lamp glowed.

Then, as his eyes got used to the dark, he gasped in horror. Looming over his town like a bad dream was a gigantic building, an edifice of granite and slate that looked as forbidding as a medieval fortress. Towers and turrets soared into the sky and battlemented walls coiled through the familiar streets like an octopus's tentacles.

In a blind panic Billy pushed against his front door, but it had shut behind him and now his key wouldn't turn in the lock. When he rushed around to the back door he found that was bolted too. Billy picked up a large stone and hurled it at its frosted glass panel.

It bounced off with a reverberating *CLANG!* The same thing happened when he tried to smash the glass in the patio door. The house was impregnable.

He had been locked out of his own home. His own world.

Overwhelmed, he sank to a heap on the doorstep. Something terrible had happened, and he hugged his knees and hid his face in the crook of his arm as his shoulders began to heave with sobs.

4

Gradually, Billy's sobs subsided to sniffling whimpers, and he wiped his nose on his sleeve and looked out across the town through swollen eyes. He saw a light, an intense fiery glow flickering in the distance. Someone had lit a beacon on top of the fortress, and flames reached into the sky, stuttering in the wind and sending a shower of sparks cascading down the fortress wall.

Billy got to his feet and stared. It was the only light in the vast blackness, and made him feel his loneliness all the more. He didn't know whether the flames were a beacon of hope or

a warning, but he had nowhere else to go. So, full of misgivings, he set off towards it.

His footsteps echoed loudly, his fear rising as he walked through the town. He passed by the cinema, its foyer empty and in darkness, and hurried by the convenience store, its doors now shut. The park gates were closed and locked, and even the all-night petrol station was in darkness. It was all so familiar and yet felt so strange – his tears threatened to start again, but he blinked them back and carried on.

He peered into the shadows ahead, his ears straining to hear the slightest sound. A Coke can suddenly rolled noisily across the pavement, making his nerves jangle, but the beacon flickering above the rooftops drew him on.

He turned into the narrow lanes that led off the High Street, and it became even darker. Billy knew this part of town well; his school was just around the corner, but now everything looked different, distorted and threatening, and his already shaky confidence wavered even more. Then something shifted in the shadows and Billy ducked behind a wall, his heart pounding.

He could make out a dark shape close to the ground, and with a shock recognized the same crawling creature he'd seen from his bedroom window. It seemed to be waiting for something. Then a group of small figures dressed in long hooded cloaks scurried from a side alley, and as they crossed the moonlit lane the creature slinked after them in close pursuit.

Billy heaved a sigh of relief, glad the crawling thing was after them and not him, but then immediately felt guilty. He wouldn't wish that nightmare creature on anyone.

Suddenly a loud clatter sounded nearby, as a jackdaw landed on a gable and began pecking at something that wriggled in its talons. With a shudder Billy gritted his teeth and carried on.

His school was threateningly dark, and he hurried by, expecting to feel something land on his shoulder or grab at his ankle at any moment. Then, turning a corner, he suddenly came upon the fortress.

Where the shopping and leisure centres should have been, where the library and town hall had once stood, an enormous fortified wall now soared up towards the sky. It was so tall Billy got a crick in his neck trying to see the top. Spires and turrets rose into clouds that scuttled across the moon like ragged ink blots, and he could hear the roar of the flaming beacon high above him.

Just ahead stood the old Corn Exchange, a building with three wide archways where Billy and his mates would sometimes meet on a Saturday, but now it was part of the fortress's

walls. Grotesque creatures were carved into the stonework and they stared malevolently down as Billy crept forward and peered through the middle arch. A line of lamps led across a quadrangle beyond and up to the castle's main entrance. Its tall doors stood wide open and a golden glow illuminated the hall inside. The soft light ahead looked so welcoming and the dark town behind so forbidding that, even though he was shaking with fear, Billy carried on across the courtyard and stepped into the fortress.

As he did so the doors slammed shut behind him. Some of the candles burning in the great central candelabra were blown out and the cavernous hall was thrown into semi-darkness. Billy ran back to the doors, but their massive iron handles were too heavy to turn. He was trapped.

With a shudder of terror he studied the hall, looking for a way out. Opposite him, two curving staircases led to a stone balcony with dark corridors leading off either end. To the left and right of him were rows of closed doors, and as Billy stood there wondering which one to try, the nearest door opened. He stepped back in surprise as a woman appeared and walked towards him, her arms spread wide.

'Aha! Another child,' she cackled in a harsh, scratchy voice, and gave Billy a lopsided smile

that looked more like a sneer. 'You're mosht welcome, I'm sure.'

She was so ancient her skin rustled like old newspapers as she moved, and her long, lank hair was covered with cobwebs and crawling with spiders. Billy stared at her stupidly and gave an involuntary shudder.

'Cat got your tongue? Hee-hee-hee,' she asked with a snigger. When Billy still didn't reply she put her bony hand on his shoulder and steered him into the side room. A counter stood at the far end, and cubbyholes stuffed with papers and books lined the wall behind.

'Shtand there,' she said, then shuffled behind the counter and climbed onto a tall stool. Billy was so scared he did exactly as he was told.

The woman reached for a large glass atomiser and sprayed herself liberally with a sickly perfume. It made Billy's eyes sting, but it wasn't strong enough to cover her musty odour. It was a stench Billy had smelled before, but he couldn't think where. Then she dragged a huge book towards her, heaved it open and peered down at him with her beady, bloodshot eyes. Billy stood transfixed.

'I am Morwella and I'm the Chief Regishtrar. And you must be . . . Billy Jones.' she said. 'It's always sho nishe to welcome new gueshts, hee-hee-hee.'

Billy opened his mouth to reply, but only made a squeak! How on earth did she know his name?

'It is Billy Jones, isn't it?' the woman snapped.

Billy nodded.

'We've been expecting you,' muttered Morwella, writing in the ledger.

'Look, I think there's been a terrible mistake,' croaked Billy, forcing himself to talk. His throat was so dry it didn't sound like him at all. 'I was on my way home from school and

must have got lost. What is this place?'

The wrinkled old wreck held up a hand for silence and continued writing. She licked her finger and turned a page, glancing up at Billy as she filled out his description, the scratchy pen spitting ink across the paper. 'Shkinny; weedy; nervoush; pliable. Just as we like 'em. Age?'

'Pardon?' stammered Billy.

'Age! How old are you?'

'Twelve,' said Billy. 'And a half.'

'Twelve,' rasped Morwella, her purple tongue protruding in concentration as she entered the number.

'And a half,' Billy muttered.

All of a sudden, Morwella leaned over the counter and grabbed Billy's arm. She turned it over, looked at the scratch on his wrist and gave a satisfied grunt.

How did she know about that? Billy wondered, as she scribbled away for a few more minutes and then slammed the book shut.

'Well, I'm sure you'll shoon shettle in,' she said, ringing a small bell on the counter.

'No!' cried Billy, almost fainting with panic. He could hear the sound of footsteps approaching. 'You don't understand. I have to get back home.'

'Thish is your home now, child, and from now on you will be known as . . . 5126,' said the old woman, checking the ledger as the door opened and the oddest-looking man loped in. He was tall and slightly stooped, with long arms that reached down to his knees. His skin was so translucent it appeared to flicker in the gloom.

'Thish is Rickett, one of our collectors,' said Morwella. 'He'll be looking after you from now on.'

'Collector?' murmured Billy, staring at the ghostly apparition. 'What do you mean – "collector"?'

'Take him to room 5126,' said Morwella.

The man tried to take Billy's hand.

'Leave off! I'm not going anywhere,' Billy cried, frantic with fear.

'Do as you're told,' growled the witchy-woman nastily. 'We don't like ungrateful little shnot-noses here.'

Rickett held out a large, spade-like hand and stared at Billy with vacant, hooded eyes. 'Coooome,' he said in a deep voice, stretching the word so it sounded as mournful as a cow lowing in the night.

'No way,' cried Billy, backing away, but the collector grabbed his wrist and pulled him into the hall. The great doors were open again, and the candelabra re-lit. As he was dragged yelling and struggling up the grand curving staircase to the high landing above, Billy heard Morwella's voice coming from the hallway below.

'What have we here – another guesht?

Hee-hee-hee,' she cackled greedily.

Billy tried to turn round and see who she was talking to, but Rickett steered him through an archway and into darkness. The air turned dank and felt charged with menace, and a soft sighing sound came from the walls as if they were alive and breathing.

The collector moved as silently as a ghost, and in the deepest shadows his transparent flesh almost entirely disappeared. His grip remained firm though, and Billy was frogmarched through a vast network of rooms that gradually grew busier and busier the further they went.

Crones like Morwella and grizzled old warlocks began to crisscross their path. They appeared from dark passages, carrying great bundles of clothes or jars of coloured gases that seemed to glow in the gloom. In one room a thousand black wire cages hung from the high ceiling, each containing a single jackdaw.

They were spookily silent, but their feathers rustled as they turned to watch Billy with their unblinking eyes, and the sound made the hair on the back of his neck stand up.

Other gangling collectors began to materialize from the shadows, some struggling with lumbering, snorting creatures they held on leashes. They were as large as Rottweilers, and sniffed at the floor like huge vacuum cleaners. One caught Billy's scent and, bellowing like an angry bear, shambled over on stubby legs, dragging a collector behind him.

Alarmed, Billy stepped back as the animal barged into him, knocking him sideways and slobbering over his shoes. It had a crumpled face and squinty little eyes that stared blindly into the darkness. Its skin was the colour of boiled liver.

'Don't mooove,' warned the collector, struggling to hold the creature back. 'Snuffler dangerooous.'

It was only then that Billy noticed the beast's long, scythe-like claws, and he froze until the growling, grunting snuffler had been hauled away. Then a collector passed by escorting a young girl, and Billy's heart leaped – suddenly he wasn't the only child in this nightmarish place.

'Hey!' he cried.

The girl turned and looked at him with pleading eyes.

'Where are . . . *ouch!*' said Billy, as Rickett squeezed his shoulder and pushed him away from the girl and into a narrow passage as dark and damp as a coal cellar. Muffled cries echoed along the passage, and Billy's skin prickled with apprehension. Then they turned a corner and he stepped out onto a metal balcony that ran around the inside of a large square tower.

Billy stopped and stared in horror. Further balconies rose above them and more dropped into the depths below. A line of sputtering torches cast each landing in an eerie glow, revealing rows of heavy doors built into the tower wall. On each landing a collector stood guard, and from behind every door came a pathetic wailing or shouting.

'What is this place?' gasped Billy. He peered over the railing into the gloomy pit below.

'Hoooome,' lowed Rickett.

'You must be joking,' cried Billy. He'd had

enough. He had to get out of there. 'No!' he yelled as Rickett reached for a key hanging by one of the doors. He kicked and wriggled, but couldn't break free from the collector's iron grip.

Rickett seemed totally indifferent to Billy's plight and his blank expression didn't change at all as he unlocked the door, pushed Billy inside and slammed it shut behind him. Billy was cast into total darkness.

'No!' Billy whimpered again, paralysed for a moment with sheer terror, and then desperately banging on the door with his fists. 'Let me out. Let me out!' he yelled, but his cries just mingled with those from the other rooms. He forced himself to step forward in the darkness, feeling his way along the wall, expecting something to grab him at any moment. But the wall felt unexpectedly smooth and Billy gradually became aware of a very familiar smell.

He couldn't place it at first. It was a rich mixture of leather wax for football boots, rotten eggs from a chemistry set and the faint pong of stale socks. And then he had it – it was the smell of his own bedroom! Feeling totally confused now, he moved further into the room and whacked his shin on something hard.

'Yeow!' he cried. He reached out and touched a low table.

This is weird, he thought. *That's just where the table is in my bedroom. But there's no way . . .*

Hardly daring to hope, Billy shuffled eagerly forward. If this were his bedroom, his bookcase would be on the left. He put out a hand, and there it was! His bed would be straight ahead. Yes! He could feel the softness of a duvet.

With a rising wave of excitement Billy swept his hand across the wall. He found the light switch, flicked it on and blinked in the sudden brightness of his own room. His heart leaped! Everything was back to normal. His toys and games were piled up in the corner; his clothes were hanging untidily out of the cupboard drawers and his gamestation stood on his desk, waiting for him to play.

He rushed over to the window, pulled back the curtain and peered out. The lights of the town glowed in the night. Car headlights moved through the streets and Billy could even hear Janus give the odd bark in the yard across the road.

'It was a nightmare,' Billy cried, tears of relief springing to his eyes. 'There is no fortress. There aren't any hags or monsters. I'm home!'

He was so pleased he hadn't called for his mum or dad; that he'd managed to deal with his fear himself. He could hear his mum now, moving about downstairs and chatting to his dad. He wanted to go and tell them about his awful dream. Dad would shake his head and ruffle his hair and Mum would give him a reassuring hug. But his terrifying ordeal had drained him, and Billy collapsed on his bed.

He was so exhausted he immediately fell into a deep, deep sleep.

5

Billy woke up, his drowsy eyes gradually bringing the room into focus. A golden glow of sunshine shone through his curtains and he smiled, snuggling into the duvet for a few more minutes. Everything was back to normal and he could put the scares of the night out of his mind.

A soft thumping noise was coming from somewhere, probably their old boiler heating the water for his bath. His dad was always promising to get a new one. Then he heard his dad singing badly to the radio downstairs, and there was a reassuring clatter just outside his door.

Oh, good, he thought, propping himself up on his elbows. His mum was bringing him a cup of hot chocolate. She always did on Saturdays, so he could have a lie-in. He usually played football, but today was Tom's birthday and he didn't want to be late.

'What's the time, Mum?' he asked, as the door opened with a squeak.

But it wasn't his mum.

'Rickett!' Billy shrieked, springing upright as the collector shuffled into his bedroom.

'Get out! Get out of my room, now!' He leaped out of bed, backing away from the lanky guard in horror. 'Dad, help!' he yelled. 'Come quick.'

Rickett looked

blankly at Billy and then stood aside so he could see through the doorway to the dark landing lined with doors.

'No!' shouted Billy, realizing he was still inside the fortress. He ran over to the window and pulled back the curtains. It was still the dead of night, and there had been no sunlight shining through them after all. In a mad panic he rushed for the door, desperate to get away, but Rickett caught him by the wrist.

'Coooome,' he mooed, and began to drag Billy towards the landing.

'Wait!' cried Billy, tears of confusion stinging his eyes. He had no idea what was going on.

Rickett looked at him with a vacant expression.

'Where am I?' asked Billy feebly.

'Hoooome,' Rickett replied,

gesturing around the room.

'This isn't my home. Please let me go. My mum and dad will be worried, and you are gonna be in so much trouble!' Billy pleaded, but Rickett grabbed him in his powerful grasp, hauled him out of the room and forced him along the landing and through the dark fortress.

They passed some blind snufflers patrolling the corridors, and a huddle of crones who stood in the middle of a room, chattering and clucking like hens.

'G'morning, 5126. Cat shtill got your tongue? Hee-hee-hee!' cackled a spiteful voice. It was Morwella. The others fell about laughing and Billy's face burned with humiliation.

He was led across wide dining halls, and through rooms that smelled as rank as farmyards. He heard fearsome growls and screams of terror coming from behind closed doors, and he grew even more scared. Then, all of a sudden, Rickett stopped and pointed down a long corridor. At the far end a door stood ajar, and a pale glow shone through the gap.

'The Briiiight Roooom,' he said, and without another word he disappeared, melding into the shadows.

'What do you mean, "the Bright Room"?' asked Billy. 'Hey, come back!'

But Rickett had already gone.

Billy couldn't believe it, and felt a spark of hope – he had been left on his own so now he could escape from the fortress! If he could get back to his house, surely he would find a way to break in . . . But glancing towards the door at the end of the passage, Billy felt an irresistible urge to find out what was on the other side.

Don't be stupid. You've got to find a way out of here, he told himself. And yet even as

this thought crossed his mind, he found he was walking down the corridor towards the Bright Room. He couldn't fight the urge to look inside.

'Surely it can't hurt to have a peek,' he reasoned. He pushed the door open and stepped into a room bathed in a soft ethereal light.

He was in a round hall with glass walls that glowed with bright angular patterns. The air seemed charged with energy, and little balls of light fizzed and popped and fell through the air like coloured rain. Just breathing the air made Billy feel calmer and happier. Then he heard a noise and turned to see a girl wander in, and his heart leaped. It was Zoe, a girl from his school – she was in the same class as him for some lessons.

'Billy?' she said. 'What's going on?'

'I've no idea, but this place is incredible,' said Billy.

Zoe gazed around the room in wonder.

'It's beautiful,' she said.

Then another child entered the room, and then two more, and Billy got the shock of his life.

'Tom!' he cried. 'How did you get here?'

'N-n-not sure,' said Tom with a nervous grin. 'I followed a cat down a passageway. I thought it was injured. When I got to the other end everything was d-d-dark, and I ended up in this fortress. Oh, Billy, I've been so scared.'

'Me too. I'm so glad to see you,' said Billy, holding up his hand for a high five. Then he recognized some of the other children coming in now – Samir and Jessica, who also went to his school.

'I wanna go home,' said a small boy Billy didn't know. He looked petrified.

'Don't worry, I'm sure we'll get home soon,' said Billy. 'And we're all together now, and this room feels safe enough.' But he didn't even convince himself. Then he noticed a scratch on the boy's wrist, and looked at the other children's hands. They all had tick-like scratches.

'Hold on a minute,' said Billy, rolling back his sleeve and showing the tick on his own wrist. 'Did you get that scratch in the Park Street shop?'

'Yes,' said the little boy. 'And it stings.'

'Me too,' said Zoe, holding out her wrist.

'And were you served by a strange old man?'

'Yeah, he was really creepy,' said Samir. 'And smelly!'

'You're right – he smelled just like Morwella. Surely that can't be a coincidence,' said Billy, screwing his face up in thought.

Suddenly there was a loud humming noise and the floor began to slowly turn beneath their feet.

'Whoa! What's happening?' cried Zoe.

A hole opened in the middle of the floor, and grew bigger and bigger as it turned. Steam billowed up as a gleaming, streamlined roller-coaster car with three rows of seats rose from the darkness below. There was a hiss of air brakes and the seats' shoulder-restraints sprang up.

'Oh wow, that's so cool!' cried Billy delightedly, as a row of lights flashed around

the seats, as if to invite them aboard. Without a moment's hesitation he clambered into the front seat of the car followed by Tom and the others, their hearts racing with expectation, all thoughts of home having melted away.

The shoulder-restraints lowered automatically and with a sudden lurch the roller coaster sprang forward and hurtled straight towards the glowing wall.

'Yahoooo!' the children yelled jubilantly, as the wall appeared to melt and their car passed through it into a long winding tube of flashing kaleidoscopic colours. The car looped the loop, throwing everyone to the left and right, and then left again.

'Woohoo!' he heard Tom cry as they shot from the end of the tube into a vast, velvety blackness. Everything went quiet. A million stars sparkled like diamonds all around them and enormous planets glowed copper and red and yellow as they spun majestically through outer space.

'Oh, wow,' gasped Billy again.

The seats' shoulder-bars hissed open and the children were tipped out of the car. Billy floated weightlessly across space. He recognized Saturn and Jupiter – they were as colourful as crystallized gumdrops – and when Billy looked down he saw the bright blue Earth beneath him. He knew his mum and dad were somewhere down there, but he was finding it difficult to think clearly about his home when he was in such a wonderful place.

His friends floated around him, smiling and wide-eyed. Billy felt he could happily stay there for ever, but with a sudden and disconcerting rush he found himself being dragged across the void at an ever-increasing pace, straight towards a gaping black hole. His body was stretched like a piece of elastic, and grew longer and longer. It was a very strange feeling being a hundred metres long, and Billy felt sure he would snap in half, but without knowing quite how it happened, he was catapulted right back into the Bright Room. The hole in the floor had disappeared and Tom and the others landed in a happy, chattering heap beside him.

'Hey, Tom, what do you think—' Billy began to say, when suddenly a row of long, ghostly tables began to appear in the room, and he fell silent. They were laden with plates of food that shimmered like holograms, and then solidified into the most wonderful feast Billy had ever seen.

'This – is – incredible!' he murmured in an awestruck whisper.

There were burgers and hot vinegary chips, sticky cakes, boxes of sugar-dusted Turkish delight, and boiled sweets that shone like jewels. There was a jam roly-poly as long as one of the tables, and a huge bowl of bright yellow custard that steamed and bubbled like a witch's cauldron.

His stomach rumbled and gurgled, and Billy realized just how famished he was. He forgot what he was going to say to Tom and rushed over, picked up a pastry and sank his teeth into it. He had never tasted anything so delicious – until he tried one of the cheeseburgers. It made his brain fizz with joy. How could anything taste so good?

Billy made his way along the table, stuffing Christmas pudding and chocolate sponge, chips dipped in ketchup and Neapolitan ice cream into his hungry mouth. There was even a birthday cake there for Tom! His friends did the same, and they let off party poppers and pulled crackers with each other, and drank fizzy drinks that seemed to set off fireworks inside their heads.

No matter how much they ate, there was

always more to try. Each mouthful was better than the one before, and by the time he'd finally had enough, Billy was feeling strangely numb. All his anger and fears had melted clean away.

'B-b-brilliant,' muttered Tom, with a slight belch as he stuffed another slice of his birthday cake in his mouth, but then the tables disappeared before their eyes and the door to the Bright Room creaked open.

Rickett and a group of other collectors entered. 'Come,' said Rickett, but Billy didn't

want to leave the enchanted room. He felt full of wonder and magic.

'Can't we stay a little longer?' he pleaded.

'Come,' repeated the other collectors, and Billy's friends trooped reluctantly out of the room.

Rickett pointed after them, his face as expressionless as a mask, and Billy grudgingly got to his feet. He was feeling so calm now he quietly followed the collector back to his room in the tower.

6

Billy sat on the edge of his bed feeling completely dazed after the magic of the Bright Room. He looked around his cell, and although he knew it was just an illusion, it was so much like his bedroom at home that he found it hard to tell what was real and what wasn't any more.

He put his hand in his pocket, hoping to find a mint to suck, but found his pocket watch instead. He took it out and looked at it – it ticked away like a little mechanical heart, but the hands didn't move and it still read four thirty. Billy sighed. It hadn't been the

good-luck charm his dad had promised, but holding the watch gave him some comfort, a connection to home, and to his mum and dad. With a mind full of questions and thoughts of escape, he crawled under his duvet and went to sleep.

He only awoke when Rickett clattered into his room the next day.

'Bright Room,' he intoned.

Billy had formed a plan to take the collector by surprise and make a mad rush for the door and for freedom – but he instantly changed his mind at the mention of the Bright Room.

I can always try and escape tomorrow, he thought, because now his only desire was to get back to that magical room.

So he dressed quickly, and obediently followed Rickett along the landing. Each of the cell doors had a little grille in the middle, and Billy glimpsed the tops of heads and frightened eyes that ducked out of sight as they passed.

When he reached the Bright Room, Tom and the others were already there.

'Hi, are you OK?' Billy asked, but they seemed a little distracted and just nodded mechanically. Even Tom seemed a little distant.

Billy didn't care – he was so eager for the magic to begin again, he didn't want to waste time talking. The next minute a huge circular hole began to open in the floor, making Billy and his friends back up until they were against the wall.

This time a large and very old-fashioned carousel rose up from below. Billy was so disappointed. The roller coaster had been incredible, but carousels were just kids' stuff. His friends were already climbing onto its wooden horses though, so he followed, and as soon as he sat down the carousel began to turn.

Billy couldn't believe it – the show was even better than before. The carousel began to spin faster, then faster and then faster still. It spun so fast the room became a blur and the prancing wooden horses snapped from their mounts and leaped high into the air. The Bright Room melted away around him, and Billy found himself galloping high above fields of golden barley. His horse raced down again, its hooves skimming a field of tulips and shaking their petals loose. The petals rose into the air as a cloud of coloured butterflies, and Billy's eyes widened in wonder. The horses galloped back to the Bright Room and Billy and his friends sprang down as they dropped into the hole in the floor. The hole closed and another magical feast appeared and Billy and his friends had a wonderful time, gorging themselves all over again. When it was time to go, Billy really didn't want to leave. He loved it in the Bright Room.

'Mooore tomorrow,' promised Rickett, so Billy obediently followed him back to his cell.

That night his dreams were a swirl of magical rides and miraculous banquets, and when he woke up he could hardly wait for Rickett to come and collect him.

* * *

Every day Billy was taken to the Bright Room, and every day the magical shows got better and better. He flew over pyramids on the back of an eagle, and lumbered through ancient ruins on a trumpeting elephant; he was transported back into the distant past and saw dinosaurs roaming the Earth; then off into a future full of strange alien beings.

At the end of each wonderful ride, a magical feast was waiting for him and his friends. The more he ate of the delicious food, the calmer Billy felt and the less he thought about his mum and dad. He could quite happily have stayed in the Bright Room for ever.

Then on the seventh day, when Billy ran into the Bright Room as usual, he noticed something that made him shudder with fear.

Tom and the others looked different! Their eyes had grown a little bigger and their skin was paler.

'Are you all right, Tom?' Billy asked. 'You look a bit, I don't know – sick.'

'Fine,' said Tom, but his voice was flat and his gaze distant. He wasn't the funny, bubbly

friend that Billy knew.

Billy touched his own face. Was he changing too? If he was, it was nothing like as quickly as his friends, but he had no idea why.

Later, as they sat at a table eating bowls of thick chocolate mousse, Billy watched in horror as Tom changed *even more*, right in front of his eyes. All the colour drained out of his friend's skin until it was a pale, muddy grey. His large eyes grew even bigger, as big and luminous as headlamps. Billy thought they might pop right out of his head.

When he looked at the others he saw they were changing quickly too. He started to panic. They were becoming so alike it was difficult to tell them apart.

'Tom!' he cried.

'I'm 5572,' said Tom, as if in a trance.

'No, you're not,' cried Billy, devastated. 'You're my best friend, Tom.'

He turned to Zoe. 'What's happening, Zoe?' he asked.

'I'm 4738,' she said flatly.

Now Billy was really scared.

'Samir?' he cried, but Samir didn't react at all. They were all just staring into space like grey-skinned automatons. Then the collectors arrived to take them back to their cells.

'What have you done to my friends?' Billy demanded, but the collectors ignored him and led the other children away. They went as meekly as lambs. 'What's happened to them?' he asked again, as Rickett led him out of the room. He wanted to kick and scream, but his brain felt muddled after the feast and he went quietly too.

Afterwards, he sat on his bed and tried to work out what was going on. He felt sure it had something to do with the magical rides and the mouth-watering food. After each trip to the Bright Room, his friends must have changed a bit more. Now they had forgotten who they were.

With a jolt of panic, he realized he couldn't remember his own name, or where he came from either, and he leaped to his feet and rushed to the mirror. His skin was paler, and his eyes were slightly bigger. He was beginning to change, just like his friends.

'Think,' he whispered, staring intently at himself. 'Who are you?' But his mind was a complete blank.

Then he heard the watch ticking in his pocket. He took it out and held it in his

hands, and a picture of his dad and his home gradually formed in his head.

'My name is Billy,' he said with a huge sigh of relief. Now he knew he must fight against the magic in the Bright Room with all his strength, or he would end up just like Tom and his friends.

* * *

When Rickett collected Billy the next day, Billy had made up his mind to resist the wonders of the Bright Room and fight the urge to gorge himself on the incredible feast. He knew if he ate too much it became difficult to think clearly, and he had realized it made it easier for Rickett to control him too. The collector no longer had to drag him around the fortress kicking and screaming, and Billy was sure the food must be laced with a terrible magic.

As he was led out of his cell, he heard the same soft thumping noise he heard every morning. His mind had always been on the Bright Room before, but now he glanced over the balcony to see what it was.

He froze with shock! The landings below were packed with shuffling lines of goggle-eyed children, just like his friends. There were hundreds upon hundreds of them; they wore long habits and stared mechanically ahead as they were marched down the spiral stairs from one landing to the next and into the depths below.

Another collector appeared on Billy's landing and began to unlock the row of doors.

A grey-skinned child appeared from each cell and shuffled past him to the stairs.

'Hey! Just a moment,' said Billy, reaching out to touch a child's arm, but they didn't even glance in his direction, and soon they had all disappeared to the landings below.

'Who were all those kids – where are they going?' Billy asked.

'The night-children,' was all Rickett said, and then hustled him quickly out of the tower.

The Magician glowered. His illusions had turned all of his new recruits into petrified night-children. All that is except one, and he desperately needed *every* child's fear to survive. For their fear was his magic. Every night-child's shiver, each of their whimpering cries, increased his power.

But now there was this one boy who had resisted his magic, as if he were protected in some way. The Magician sensed that gaining his fear would give him the most power of all, and he knew he must redouble his efforts.

7

This time, none of Billy's friends came to the Bright Room, and he knew they must have joined the hordes of children he'd seen in the tower. Now Billy was truly alone, and really, really scared. Then when the show started, he became petrified!

This time the magic was very different. There was no kaleidoscope of wonderful colours; no roller-coaster rides or galloping horses, and no field of tulips that turned into butterflies. Instead the walls darkened and seemed to billow and boil like storm clouds. Flashes of light crackled inside them as a strong wind started to blow. It lifted Billy up and threw him against the wall.

'Ooof!' Billy cried, dropping to the ground and covering his ears as the wind howled and the thunder crashed.

Now the floor opened again and a flock of grotesque little gargoyles flew out, like a colony of squealing bats. They spun around Billy's head, howling like lost souls as lightning snaked from the walls, crackling with electricity and booming with thunderclaps that echoed round and around the room.

'Stop!' Billy screamed, but the little grinning monsters whirled ever closer to his face, snapping and spitting. 'PLEASE STOP!'

And they stopped . . . and everything was silent, and the screaming monsters melted into a dark fog that shifted and rolled, forming an immense figure – a featureless silhouette as tall as a giant and as faint as vapour. It only lasted a few seconds before the shape dispersed, but Billy recognized it instantly and a shiver of terror ran down his spine. It was the figure he'd seen at his bedroom window – the figure with the creeping creature at its feet.

'What do you want with me?' Billy cried, tears starting to stream down his cheeks. 'Please let me go home. My mum will be worried.'

The fog whipped around the room and rolled up to the ceiling, creating a draught that sounded like a whisper.

'At last. You're my child now,' it seemed to

say. 'A night-child
– look!'

A mirror of light formed in front of Billy. He could see himself quite clearly, and let out a horrified gasp. His eyes were big and staring and his skin was as grey as Tom's. Despite his determination to resist the Bright Room's magic, he had become just like his friends.

'No!' he whimpered. 'Turn me back. Turn me back now!'

A laugh rolled through the air like a buffeting wind, and the fog grew and grew and flattened out like a huge dark sheet that filled the room. Billy could see pinpoints of light glimmering in the blackness, and the tail of a shooting star. Then the darkness was gone, and Billy found himself back in the soft comforting glow of the Bright Room once more.

A banqueting table had appeared, but this time there was only a single slice of cake on it – but oh, what a cake it was! Large as a loaf and oozing with honey so dark it was almost black. The sweet smell filled Billy's nostrils and swirled around his brain. He knew if he took a bite he would be lost for ever, but he

couldn't help himself and he lifted the cake up to his mouth.

Then somewhere in his subconscious, Billy became aware of the faintest ticking.

Tick-tock, tick-tock, tick-tock.

It was his pocket watch. He looked at the delicious cake . . . and listened to the ticking . . . and looked at the cake again. Then with a cry of desperation he threw the cake across the room, plunged his hand into his pocket and gripped the watch tight. It filled his mind with memories of home. He remembered what his dad had said about the pocket watch, and felt a new strength flow into him. His appearance might have changed, but he could still think for himself and he knew he had to escape while he had some fight left in him.

The door opened behind him and Rickett entered the Bright Room.

'Come,' he droned, and Billy let himself be led back to his cell, his mind buzzing with ideas.

The collector took the key to Billy's room from its nail, unlocked the door and pushed him inside. Billy heard the key turn in the lock again, but didn't mind – he had the inkling of a plan that could change everything.

8

Billy rummaged through his chest of drawers. They were full of the odds and ends he kept in his real room – broken toys, old coins, and things he thought might come in handy. He grabbed an old pair of pliers and the rear-view mirror that had snapped off the handlebars of his bike, and went over to his wardrobe.

As he reached for a coat hanger Billy's head began to swim, and he flopped down in a heap on the bed. His mind was blank, and for a moment he forgot what he had been doing. He shook his head, took a few deep breaths and gradually began to feel better.

If I don't get out soon, it'll be too late, he thought, and struggled to his feet.

He took the wire coat hanger from the wardrobe and, using the pliers, unwound it and stretched it out. He made a hook at one end, then went over to the door and looked through the small, barred peephole. There was nobody on the landing.

'Perfect,' he whispered, and poked the wire through the bars. He couldn't see the key, so he held the mirror at an angle until he could see its reflection. The wire wobbled and twitched as Billy slowly manoeuvred the hooked end towards it.

'Gently does it,' he whispered – then Rickett appeared at the far end of the landing and Billy whipped the wire back inside his room.

'What the heck does he want?' he muttered, ducking below the little window.

The impassive collector slowly patrolled the landing, marching back and forth and stopping occasionally to peer into a cell. Billy thought he would never clear off, but eventually he disappeared back down the staircase to the floors below.

Billy tried again. It was like playing 'Hook-A-Duck' at the fairground, with everything reversed in a mirror. The wire trembled and quivered, but this time he managed to hook the key. Very carefully he lifted it from the nail and pulled it back

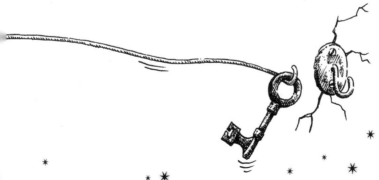

towards him.

'Got it!' he whispered, clutching the key in his hand. Then, hardly daring to breathe, he placed it in the lock. It turned with a clunk and the door creaked open.

Billy sneaked along the landing, peering nervously over the railings to the floors below. He could see collectors prowling some of the other landings, but for the moment his floor was clear. With his nerves jangling he darted out of the tower, along the damp corridor, and tiptoed silently into the room of jackdaws.

He could hear their feathers rustle as he sneaked across the floor, desperate not to rouse them. Then, just as he thought he was going to make it, one of the birds spotted him and screeched out loud.

'*Carck! Carck!*'

Now the other birds started – '*Carck-carck-carck*' – and soon the room was full of gossiping bird calls. Billy ran as fast as he

could across the hall, and as he dived into the next room he heard the squeaks of a thousand rusty cages opening, and a great flapping noise as the jackdaws swooped down from the ceiling.

'*Urgh!*' He skidded to a halt. Now he could see the shadow of a figure in a doorway at the other end of the room. He didn't know which way to turn!

Then, as the jackdaws flew in behind him

like sheets of raggedy paper, he dived behind a stack of old chairs piled higgledy-piggledy along one wall.

Two large jackdaws landed right next to him and fixed him with their gimlet eyes.

'Psst. Clear off!' Billy whispered urgently, but they ignored him and cocked their heads on one side.

Peering between the tangle of chair legs,

Billy saw Morwella appear in the far doorway holding a flickering candelabra, and he hunkered further back in the shadows. Three other witchy figures followed her, each with a bulging sack in their hand.

'Shoo,' cackled Morwella, as the jackdaws flapped around her. 'Get back to your cages, you wicked things!'

'Somezink has got zem rattled. Maybe iz a night-child,' grunted a warlock with a thick accent and a voice as rough as sandpaper. He had long white hair, a sharp, warty nose and wore a black eyepatch.

Billy crouched even lower in the shadows.

'Let'sh find out shall we, Jashper?' said Morwella, giving a wide, toothless grin and scratching her hairy chin. 'You take that shide of the room, and I'll shearch this shide. If there's anyone in here, I'll grind 'em to paste and shpread 'em on my toasht.' Then, turning to the others, she screeched, 'Shnotnose,

Broadshanks, get the birds back in their cages and get them fed.'

The two birds near Billy hopped closer. He blew at them, hoping they would fly off, but they just stared at him even harder. Then Billy spotted a hard piece of chewing gum stuck to the underside of one of the chairs. He picked it off and flicked it hard. It ricocheted off one bird and whacked the other, and they rose squawking into the air. Luckily, at that moment, all the other birds started to screech too as Snotnose and Broadshanks carried their sacks past Billy's hiding place, dribbling trails of birdseed in their wake. Like a churning black cloud, the jackdaws followed.

But the danger wasn't over yet – Morwella began walking the length of the room, peering into the stack of furniture, and Jasper did the same the other side. Billy held his breath, not daring to move as Morwella passed close by, then stopped in her tracks. Billy thought his heart might burst through his chest, it was beating so hard. A fat spider dropped from Morwella's hair as her large, watery eyes stared at him through the chair legs.

'Is there shomebody in there?' she croaked in a sing-song voice, sniffing the air with her snub nose and raising the candles over her head. 'Come out, my shweetie, whoever you are.'

She shuffled one way and then the other, staring into the gloom. Billy's lungs started to burn – he couldn't hold his breath much longer!

'Zere iz nussink my side,' growled Jasper, joining Morwella. Now both witches were so close Billy could have reached out and touched them. He was sure they must see him, but with a grunt Morwella lowered the candelabrum.

'Nothing here, either. It was jusht a trick of the light,' she said.

'We should shift all zese chairs and have a

proper look,' suggested Jasper.

'We haven't got time for that,' said Morwella. 'Letsh go!'

And to Billy's huge relief they waddled off towards the hall of jackdaws. He hurried out of the room in the opposite direction, and into a long, cobwebby corridor. Flaming torches provided only a weak light and the walls dripped with a sticky dampness. It soon became so cold Billy could see his breath cloud in the gloom.

He didn't know where he was going – he just wanted to find a way out of the fortress. Then if he could get back inside his house everything might return to normal, and he would find his mum and dad waiting for him. He pressed on, but the corridor divided into a labyrinth of narrow passages and before long Billy knew he had become hopelessly lost.

The passages all looked the same, and with a growing horror he realized he could be lost for ever. The only sound he could hear was his own breathing, the slow echoing drip of water, and then a sniffling, snorting noise that made him stop in his tracks. He recognized it at once, and with a shudder of horror he spun around and saw two large snufflers appear out of the darkness.

Billy turned and ran. The creatures lifted their heads, sniffed the air and, bellowing loudly, shuffled after him, their deadly claws

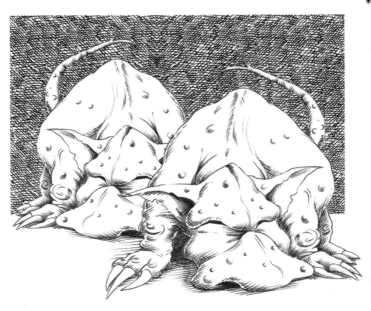

clattering on the ground. He could easily outrun them, but the corridors grew so dark he had to slow to a crawl and feel his way along. His fear of the dark flooded through him and he started to panic.

Suddenly he heard a horrible, throaty wheezing coming from the opposite direction.

'We've got you, boy!' came a familiar taunting voice. 'You might as well shurrender. Hee-hee-hee!'

Morwella!

Billy could see a flaming torch in the distance. Then all of a sudden, the snufflers were upon him, forcing him back against the wall and grunting and snorting like giant hogs.

'Shtay right where you are,' screeched Morwella, and Billy's heart sank as she hobbled up to him and fixed him with a cold stare. The taunting face of Jasper appeared at her shoulder.

'I knew zere waz zomeone on the loose,' he

sneered.

Billy felt devastated, and raised his shaking hands in the air.

'OK. I surrender,' he said, his voice flat with defeat. But as Jasper reached out to grab hold of him, Billy was yanked backwards into the blackest shadows.

'Oh!' he cried.

'Where's he gone?' he heard Morwella screech.

'This way!' whispered a girl's voice in Billy's ear, and she gripped his hand and dragged him into a corridor so dark and narrow he hadn't even seen it was there.

'Let'sh get after him!' screeched Morwella, but the snufflers and the witches were too wide to squeeze into the narrow gap. 'Come back, you shnotty-nosed blighter!'

* * *

Billy let himself be led blindly through the dark. Soon the corridor opened out, and his

unknown rescuer broke into a run, dragging Billy behind her. He could hear other footsteps running alongside him. They turned this way then that, and the growling and screeching grew fainter and fainter. When they finally came to a stop under a glowing wall light Billy saw his rescuers were three grey-skinned, goggle-eyed children – a girl and two boys.

'Thanks,' he said, panting hard. 'Who are you?'

'We'll explain later,' said the girl. 'Just follow us,'

Billy had no idea where they were going but he felt like he could trust these night-children, and followed them along deserted corridors and down into a deep, dank cellar that looked as if it hadn't been used for years. Here, a secret door in the wall opened into an underground tunnel that led them deeper and deeper into the earth. A score of other tunnels joined it and branched off from it, and it grew narrower and narrower as they scurried along. It was as convoluted as a termite mound and Billy began to feel increasingly claustrophobic. But just as he was starting to get really jittery the tunnel widened and he stepped into a large cave bathed in a faint, shimmering light.

9

Billy was transfixed by the scene before him. Large stalagmites rose from the cavern floor and stalactites hung from the high ceiling. Some met in the middle, creating milky white columns that seemed to glow in the gloom.

The wall opposite was dotted with dark holes, like a huge slab of cheese. Inside were cushions and blankets, and he guessed each hole must be a tiny bedroom. It all looked so welcoming after the darkness of the tunnels, and he immediately felt reassured.

A long, rickety table stood in the centre of

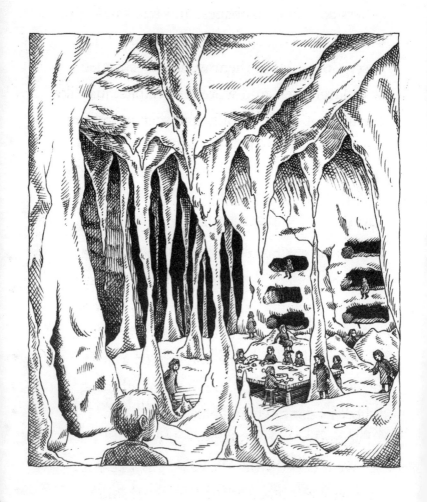

the cavern with about ten other night-children sat around it – a couple were peeling potatoes; others chopping cabbages, and one small girl seemed to be fixing the workings of a large, rusty clock. All of them were grey-skinned with large eyes, and wore long habits, just like the lines of children Billy had seen marching along the cell block landings.

'Welcome to our lair. My name's Lightning,' said the girl. She was still holding his hand and Billy self-consciously pulled it free. Then, indicating the boys who had helped rescue him, she added, 'And this is Ace and Dusty. You'll soon get to know the other Runners.'

'Hi,' said Ace, with a friendly grin. He had a smiling, freckled face and looked a little older than the others, but it was Lightning who was definitely in charge.

'Runners?' said Billy, perplexed.

'We escaped from the cells, just like you, and we call ourselves the Runners,' said

Lightning. 'What's your name?'

'Billy,' said Billy. He realized everyone was staring at him, and he suddenly felt awkward under their silent gaze. His cheeks started to blush with colour.

'Are you 'ungry?' asked a boy. He had a shrill voice and an incredibly grubby face.

Billy nodded. His adventures had made him famished. 'You bet. I could eat a horse, um – what's your name?'

'You can call me Grubby,' said the boy. 'Everyone else does.'

Billy sat down at the table and Grubby brought him a bowl of thick potato soup, dished up from a deep pot over a roaring fire.

'It's not an 'orse, but it should fill yer up!' he said with a chuckle, and when Billy looked up to say thanks, he found all the Runners staring back at him with wide friendly grins. He began to feel a little more confident.

'Thanks for rescuing me,' he said between spoonfuls of delicious soup.

'That's OK. It's what we do,' said Lightning.

'But how did you know where I was?'

'We didn't! We were out scavenging, looking for food and stuff, when we heard the bellowing of a snuffler. We knew someone must be in trouble so we came running.'

'The snufflers were after you?' asked Grubby, with a shudder. 'I hate them things – they chase me through all my worst nightmares.'

'It's horrible dreams about witches that make me wake up screaming,' said the small girl who had been working on the old clock, her squeaky voice shaking with fear.

'The fortress is teeming with terrible creatures, and each one is somebody's worst nightmare,' explained Lightning. 'Like witches for Compass there, and snufflers for Grubby. You were lucky we got to you when we did, otherwise you'd have been hauled before the Magician.'

At the mention of a magician, a spasm of fear jolted Billy. 'Who's he?' he asked, his voice suddenly dry and croaky, but he already knew the answer. It had to be the terrifying figure he'd glimpsed in the Bright Room.

'He's the supreme ruler of this whole dark world. This is *his* fortress, and all the other creatures are just his lowly minions,' said Lightning, her eyes as clear and bright as two new marbles. 'They keep the night-children under control, doing the Magician's bidding.'

'Yeah, they force the kids to build more

rooms and higher towers to the fortress, but the Magician is never satisfied. He always wants more,' said Ace. 'It's a back-breaking job, and it never ever ends.'

'Blimey!' murmured Billy, realizing what had been in store for him if he hadn't managed to escape.

'We're better off than most, though. At least we know we don't come from here,' said Lightning, pursing her lips in thought. 'All the other night-children think this fortress is their real home! Their brains have been frazzled by the Magician's magic – we escaped before the Bright Room fully changed us. We got chatting amongst ourselves and planned our escape. We broke out of the cells and ended up here.'

'So, why haven't you gone home?' asked Billy, utterly astonished.

'Home?!'

'Yes, why—'

'Don't you think we would if we could?'

snapped Lightning, and Billy saw tears well up in her large, luminous eyes. 'Course we would. We can get out and go into the town – but none of us can remember where our real home is, or what it was like. We can't even remember our proper names!'

'Oh! Sorry,' mumbled Billy, feeling terrible. There was an awkward silence as the Runners stared into space, lost in their own thoughts.

'What about you,' Grubby asked him, breaking the silence at last. He wiped his nose on the back of his sleeve, leaving a new streak of dirt on his cheek. 'Can you remember anything about your 'ome?'

'Well, yes . . . I can,' said Billy cautiously, not sure how they would react.

'Oh, really? And what makes you so different?' asked Ace, a little belligerently.

Billy shrugged. 'I dunno,' he said. 'But I reckon it's got something to do with *this*.' And he took out his pocket watch and laid it on the table.

'Oh, wow,' said Lightning, her large eyes shining with wonder. 'That's amazing. What does it do?'

'Well, my dad said it would protect me,' said Billy. 'But I don't know how it works.'

'Mind if I . . . ?' asked Compass, excitedly reaching for the watch.

'Help yourself,' said Billy.

Compass snapped the back off the watch and unscrewed the top plate. 'Let's have a look

at its workings,' she said. But when she lifted the plate, there was nothing inside the watch at all. No cogs or springs or wheels. 'I think your dad must've been having you on,' she said. 'This couldn't work in a month of Sundays.'

Billy was shocked. 'But it does go – I've seen the hands move,' he said. 'And I do remember my home, and how I got here too.'

'Really?' said Lightning, her nose creasing in disbelief.

'Sure – I got home from school one day and my house was deserted, except for a trapped jackdaw—'

'Jackdaws are some of the Magician's familiars,' interrupted Lightning earnestly.

'It attacked me, and when I rushed outside everything was dark,' continued Billy. 'If I can only retrace my steps and get back inside my house, I'm sure things will return to normal.'

'Yeah, right,' muttered a Runner with long cornrowed hair.

'It's true,' insisted Billy, and he told them all about his home and his mum and dad and the school he went to. The Runners couldn't believe their ears, and a ripple of excitement passed through them.

'If we came with you and got into your real life, do you think we would get home too? Back to our own real lives?' asked Lightning.

'I don't know, but it's got to be worth a try, hasn't it?' said Billy.

Compass squeaked with excitement.

'There's a problem, though – my house is locked up tight. I tried to get back inside, but it was impossible,' Billy explained.

'Don't worry about that,' smiled Ace. 'I'm an expert lock-picker, and there isn't a door I 'aven't managed to open yet!'

'Brilliant. What are we waiting for – let's go now!' said Billy jumping to his feet, hardly able to contain himself. Compass and Nipper, her friend with the cornrowed hair, were carried away on a wave of excitement too, and began to chant.

'We're going home, we're going home,' they sang.

Then, pausing to think for a moment, Compass asked, 'But what if we get back to our real world and still can't remember where our own houses are? What if it's nowhere near our homes at all?'

'We'll cross that bridge when we come to it,' said Lightning. 'Let's escape from this dark place first.' She turned to Billy and gave him a serious look. 'You're sure about this, Billy?' she asked. 'It's dangerous going out into the town, and we need to be sure it's worth the risk.'

'I'm sure,' said Billy, though he wasn't feeling as confident as he sounded.

'Excellent! So where do you live?'

'On Merlin Place, up on the ridge above the park.'

'Then our best route will be through the

badgers' sett,' she said. 'It will take us to the far side of town.'

'Hold on,' said Ace. 'Don't you think Billy should change out of those weird clothes first?'

Billy looked at his sweatshirt and jeans. 'Weird?' he asked.

'He's right. The watch creatures are always on the lookout for Runners, and in those clothes you'll stand out like a sore thumb. Get him a gown, Grubby,' said Lightning.

Grubby dragged an old night-child's gown from a chest in the corner, and Billy pulled it on over his clothes. It was heavy and felt rather itchy, even through his sweatshirt.

'OK?' he asked, feeling slightly daft.

'Perfect,' said Lightning. 'Now, let's go.'

Billy followed Lightning to a corner of the cave where a flight of rough-hewn steps led further down into the ground. Jiggling with nervous energy the Runners pushed and jostled behind him.

'We're going home, we're going home,' chanted Compass again.

'Sshh!' ordered Lightning. 'Everyone keep your noise down.'

The Magician, a brooding, swirling dark fog, was in his apartment at the top of the great fortress's keep. Across the table stood a werehound, one of his elite guards. It was a fearsome creature with wild eyes set in shaggy, matted fur that had moulted in great chunks, leaving the top part of its muzzle bare to the bone. In front of the Magician, though, the werehound cowered like a street mongrel.

'Gone?' enquired the Magician in a menacing whisper, his misty shape ballooning upwards to loom threateningly over the hound before sinking back again.

'Yes, s-sir. S-sorry, sir,' whimpered the hound. 'The witches nearly caught him, but – waaooow! – he got away.'

'Who was looking after him?' asked the Magician, and the air around him rumbled like thunder.

'Grrr-Rickett, sir,' said the werehound, shaking uncontrollably.

'Punish him,' the Magician hissed, his shifting dark shape sparking and flashing with energy. 'Punish him now!'

CRACK! A bolt of lightning zipped across the room and sent the hound scurrying out of the door.

On his own again, the Magician's vaporous shape became focused,

solidifying into a towering, angular man with a face as hard and sharp as a hatchet. With a scowl he opened the ledger on his desk and ran a finger down the margin. 5126 – so, it was that child again. Despite his best efforts, the quivering wretch had still not conformed. Just like the others it was fear that had brought him here, and if anything, his fear was stronger than most – but his spirit had not been broken. He still remembered too much. Why was that – what made him tick?

The Magician smashed his fist onto the table and hissed like a giant serpent. 5126 must be recaptured, and then he would be taught a lesson he would never forget. He needed all the night-children's sad and pathetic fears, but now, more than ever, he wanted this child's fear. With a grin of pure malice, he dissolved back into the darkness.

10

Billy kept close to Lightning as they crept through the badgers' sett. It led deep beneath the courtyards of the sprawling fortress and smelled musty, like the elephant house at a zoo. In places it became so low he had to crawl on all fours, shuffling past straw-filled chambers where the badgers slept. Billy was sure two beady eyes stared back at him from amongst the bedding.

The rest of the Runners followed on behind, bickering excitedly until Lightning had to tell them to be quiet once more. Then, pushing past a tangle of roots protruding from the earth, the tunnel began to climb and Billy emerged from a hole in a ramshackle garden in the town.

He peeped over the garden wall. The street was full of creeping shadows cast by a waxy moon, but he recognized it as Shipton Road.

'OK, I know where we are. Follow me,' he called in a hushed whisper, and led the motley crew through the empty town, swallowing his fear as he peered nervously around corners before dashing across deserted streets. He

knew every building, and even though they looked distorted and threatening in the dark, he somehow half expected to see someone he knew walk casually around a corner. Here was the coffee shop his mum always visited when they went shopping in town; there the bargain store, usually thronged with people; opposite was the spot where the homeless man sold magazines, but it was empty apart from the little square of cardboard where his scruffy dog usually sat.

Billy strained his ears for the sound of a car purring along a nearby road, or for the chimes of the town clock. But the clock was stopped and the streets as empty as a ghost town. Not an owl hooted, not a tomcat yowled. There were no sounds of footsteps, of voices calling out, or police cars wailing. It was so quiet, Billy was sure he could hear his own heart beating. Even though the Runners were with him, he felt scared and vulnerable, and it made him want to yell at the top of his voice: 'Is anybody there?'

Finally, they arrived at his house on Merlin Place.

'This is it!' he whispered to the excited Runners.

The driveway was crisscrossed by shadows, and the gravel crunched under their feet as they crept towards Billy's house. The bushes on either side rustled in the night breeze.

Billy ducked into the porch, lifted the flap of the letter box and peered inside. His house was still deserted, and it made him feel like a stranger, as if he didn't belong there. Hoicking up the skirt of his robe, he dug down into his jeans pocket, found his key and inserted it into the lock. It wouldn't turn.

'There, you see? It's locked solid,' he whispered. 'Back door's the same too.'

'It must be deadlocked, but that's no problem. I can easily get around that,' said

Ace, taking a rolled-up pouch from his pocket. He opened it and chose two long tools from a row of lock picks.

'Cool!' said Billy.

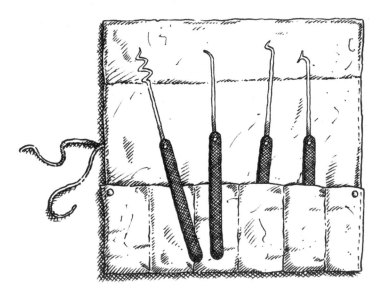

'Right, I need complete silence,' said Ace, cracking his knuckles like a safebreaker and inserting the picks into the lock. 'Mmm, this is a tricky one,' he added, his ear resting against the door.

Billy watched impatiently as the boy

twiddled and turned the picks. It was taking ages, and he became more and more impatient as the seconds ticked by. Ace grimaced and took a finer tool from his pouch. Eventually, with a grunt of frustration, he gave up.

'It's no good,' he said. 'I can't do it!'

'You're joking!' cried Billy. He was devastated. The thought he might not be able to get home was almost too much to bear, and all his frustrations and fears came rushing to the surface.

'You weren't trying hard enough! Let me have a go,' he yelled, but without warning Ace spun him round and clamped a hand firmly over his mouth.

'Mmm, mmm, mmm!' protested Billy.

'Quiet!' whispered Ace. 'Crawlers!'

To his horror Billy saw three figures slink into his driveway. They were the same as the nightmare creature that had visited his bedroom – little wild-haired men with jagged teeth as sharp as a shark's, and just the sight of them made his stomach turn.

The crawlers momentarily disappeared behind some shrubs, and Billy found himself being dragged out of the porch and behind the thick foliage of a nearby hedge at the side of the house.

'Quick, everyone, behind here!' whispered Lightning.

The creatures reappeared and crept towards them, hissing like leaking boilers. Billy's chest tightened with panic as the little crawling men climbed the steps into the porch and began sniffing about, their noses gurgling with

mucus. They were just a couple of metres away and he knew it was only a matter of seconds before they were discovered.

This mission had been Billy's idea, and now everyone was in danger. It was up to him to do something about it. Silently, and with shaking hands, he picked up a large stone from the flower bed and flung it towards the back garden.

The crawlers jumped as the stone clattered through the undergrowth beyond, and scurried over to the tall iron gate that led into the back. As they peered eagerly through the bars they were only a couple of steps away, and Billy held his breath as he carefully picked up another stone and threw it high over the gate. This time it hit his mum's greenhouse, and there was a crash of breaking glass. With excited yelps the crawlers flung the gate open and raced through it.

'Run for it,' Billy whispered, his voice

hoarse with fear, and as the gang hurried off down the drive he darted up to the gate, pushed it shut and turned its rusty key. He breathed a sigh of relief – but a crawler's thin pale arm snaked back between the bars. It grabbed Billy's wrist and yanked him towards the gate, and his head hit it with a resounding clang.

He slumped to the ground, dazed. Another crawler joined in, pulling Billy so close to the gate his face was tight against the bars – only centimetres away from the crawler's snarling,

spitting mouth!

'Get off!' Billy yelled, but the crawler opened its jaws to reveal a row of sharp, triangular teeth. Then, giggling like a crazed hyena, it bit down on his arm.

'Aargh!'

Suddenly a heavy branch was driven between the bars and hit the crawler hard on the forehead. It let go with a scream, and scurried off into the garden, holding a bleeding wound. Billy looked up to see Lightning standing above him, wielding the branch like a battering ram.

Whack! She drove it into the stomach of the second crawler, and it gasped and leaped back, retching noisily. But the third crawler jumped at the gate and started to climb as effortlessly as a monkey. In a second it was atop the gate and grinning down at Billy and Lightning.

'Watch out,' yelled a high-pitched voice, and Billy saw the short round figure of Compass running towards them. As she passed a moss-covered birdbath, she lifted its bowl free and hurled the contents at the crawler. The water hit the creature full in the face. It lifted its hands to its eyes and started to yowl, dropping back into the garden and writhing on the ground.

'Run!' yelled Billy, scrambling to his feet, and they ran down the drive and out on the street to join the other Runners. The whole gang took to their heels and pelted down the road, turning into side alleys and back streets, and didn't stop until they were convinced the crawlers hadn't followed them.

'How on earth did you know they hated water?' Billy asked Compass. He was still shaking from a surge of adrenaline.

'I didn't,' said Compass. 'I meant to hit it with the birdbath!'

'It did the trick, anyway,' grinned Lightning. 'We'll have to remember that for the future.

How's your arm, Billy?'

Billy pulled the sleeve of his tunic up and looked at his forearm. There was a row of indentations in his flesh from the crawler's teeth, but the fabric of the tunic was thick and his skin hadn't been broken.

'I'll live. Look, I'm really sorry I got your hopes up – and put your lives in danger too,' he said.

'Don't worry, we should have told you there'd be crawlers about. It's their job to patrol the streets,' said Lightning, and gave him a reassuring smile. 'You sure you're OK?'

Billy nodded.

'Then let's do some scavenging, whilst we're here. Come on.'

Billy followed her down a narrow street that led to the little row of shops near the park. He knew this part of town really well, but when the gang squeezed between the bars of the park gates, he stopped in amazement.

It was almost unrecognizable. Gone were the swings and slides, the football pitch and the skate park he knew so well. Now, every square metre was given over to growing vegetables.

Billy hunkered down behind a park bench with the others.

'Has everyone got their scavenging bags with them?' whispered Lightning.

The others nodded, pulling canvas sacks from the deep pockets in their gowns.

'I haven't,' said Billy.

'Never mind. You stay here and keep a lookout. The crawlers are bound to be looking for us now. If you see any, just whistle.'

'Er, yeah, OK,' he said, a little uncertainly. He didn't want to be left alone in the windswept darkness, but he wasn't going to show he was afraid.

They were gone in a flash, and Billy crouched behind the bench and surveyed the bewildering scene. Before him the vegetable

plots disappeared into the dusky distance; to his right was a row of familiar houses from his town; but over to the left the black fortress rose high into the dark sky. A new tower was being built, and hundreds of night-children were moving over it like worker ants, hauling up blocks of stone on pulleys and swinging them into place. Billy was glad he wasn't one of them.

Minutes ticked by, and he began to get edgy. He could hear the rustling of wind through the crops and the snorting of unseen night creatures, but he couldn't see his friends anywhere. Suddenly, half a dozen crawlers appeared in the distance. They began to creep up and down the paths between the vegetable beds, peering eagerly amongst the foliage.

'Uh-oh!' Billy whispered to himself. He puckered his lips, ready to whistle a warning, but they were so dry he only managed to blow a raspberry. He caught a glimpse of the Runners in the moonlight, halfway across the park – tiny figures dashing along the rows of beans. He wet his lips and tried again, emitting a warbling trill. The Runners dropped to the ground as if they'd been shot and Billy watched nervously as the crawlers moved closer and closer to where they had been.

He heard a distant hiss as a crawler waded in amongst the vegetables, frantically sweeping their leaves aside, and then stooping to grab something.

'They've been caught!' gasped Billy.

Then a hand tapped him on the shoulder and he nearly jumped out of his skin. He turned to see the grinning face of Lightning. The Runners had returned as silently as cat burglars, their home-made bags bulging with pilfered vegetables.

Billy gave a huge sigh of relief, and without another word they set off for their lair deep below the fortress.

11

Although it was always dark in this strange world, the Runners still called the time they slept 'night' and the time they were awake 'day', and they were up and busy from early the next morning.

Billy was feeling wretched, though. He was desperate to escape from the darkness and get home, but now he didn't know if it would ever be possible. If Ace – an expert at picking locks – couldn't break into his house, what chance did he himself have?

'You OK, Billy?' asked Lightning as she passed by, carrying an armful of kindling wood.

'Yeah, fine,' said Billy, shaking himself out of his mood. 'Can I help?'

'You could get some more wood from the store and bring it over to the fire,' she said and, always eager to help, Billy hurried off to the smaller cave where the Runners stored their finds – food and wood, and paper and pens, and pots and scissors and tools.

The others joked happily with him as they prepared their meal and fed the fire with wood scavenged from the fortress bins. They swept the floor, made their beds and washed up the dirty plates from the night before. Billy tried to help, but he was soon getting in everyone's way, so he sat down at the table and began to rummage through its long rickety drawer. It was stuffed full with all sorts of odds and ends – broken knives, bent forks and cogs and wheels from the clock that Compass still worked on when she had the time.

At the back of the drawer Billy found three dusty old notebooks. Curious, he took them out and opened the first one. The paper had yellowed and become brittle with age.

This is the very first meeting of

The Magnificent Runners!

We've escaped from our cells and are on the run from the Magician and his familiars. No more being bossed by witches and warlocks! No more being terrorized by crawlers and jackdaws!

Our Aims:
1. Help other night-children escape from their cells and join us.
2. Do everything we can to disrupt the life of the fortress by worrying the witches, confounding the collectors! and ambushing the snufflers.

> 3. Find a way to leave the Magician's dark world forever and get back to our homes — wherever they may be.
>
> Signed by:
> Weasel, Dozy, Fleetfoot, Sniffer, Brains, Stink and Fearless.

'What are these?' he asked Ace, who was struggling past with a bag full of corncobs for the cooking pot.

'Oh, they're the logbooks of the *original* Runners,' said Ace. 'This must 'ave been their hideout at one time, because those books were already here when we discovered this place.

We decided we'd call ourselves Runners too, and try 'n' help others escape, just like them.'

'What happened to them?' asked Billy.

'No idea – they were long-gone when we got here,' said Ace, as he dragged the sack of corncobs off to the fire.

How long ago had the original Runners lived here? Billy wondered. *For how many years had this dark fortress existed?*

He continued to flick through the notebooks, but most of them were just filled with lists of things the Runners had scavenged. Then, as he turned a page in the final book, Billy sat up and his heart leaped with excitement.

'Hey, Lightning, have you read this?' he asked, rushing over to where she was drawing water from an underground well. Without waiting for an answer, he began reading the entry out loud:

> Fleetfoot has gone missing! We found this note on her pillow:
>
> > Fellow Runners, I have some mind-bending news – I've discovered overwhelming evidence that somewhere in this fortress, is a weapon SO POWERFUL it can defeat the MIGHTY MAGICIAN himself. I have gone to search for it. Hold on to your hats – this could be the answer to all our problems!
>
> Oh, dear! This sounds like another of Fleetfoot's madcap schemes, and we hope she returns safe and sound.

'What do you think?' Billy asked, thrilled by his find.

'Yeah, we've seen it,' said Lightning, and he was astonished by her seeming indifference. 'Have you read the last page?'

Billy turned to the end of the book and as he began to read, his heart sank.

> A year has passed, and Fleetfoot hasn't returned. We've sent out countless search parties, but there is no sign of her, or of any weapon. She must have been taken prisoner — or worse.

'Oh,' said Billy, with a sigh of disappointment.

'We've looked as well, Billy, but we didn't find anything either,' said Lightning. 'No one knows what happened to Fleetfoot, or any of the other original Runners.'

'Maybe they got home,' suggested Billy, though he knew they had probably been recaptured.

Then someone yelled, 'Grub's up!' and he was nearly knocked over as the Runners stampeded for the table. Billy watched in astonishment as they pushed and shoved and grabbed at buttery corncobs, hot potatoes and slices of roast ham and, not wanting to miss out, he pushed his way in amongst them!

Nobody bothered with knives and forks, it saved on the washing-up, and anyway it was much more fun to eat with your hands! Billy had to be quick, though – the Runners stuffed their mouths full while chattering away like monkeys, and in no time at all there was nothing left. It was like feeding time at the zoo!

In the afternoon some of the Runners went out scavenging – creeping all over the fortress and bringing back anything that might be useful. Billy stayed in their lair washing pots, all the while thinking of ways he could escape the dark world and wondering if he ever would.

'You can come with us tomorrow, if you like,' said Compass later, as Billy watched her empty her scavenging bag onto the table after a successful haul. He was amazed at the things she'd managed to find – a bottle opener, a box of matches, a mop head, a fountain pen, a table lamp, a kettle with a hole in it and a potato peeler with a broken handle.

'Sure,' said Billy, feeling pleased that he felt brave enough to go sneaking around the fortress.

The last few days of excitement had caught up with him now though, and he gave such a yawn that he thought the top of his head might drop off. He climbed up to the hole in the wall where his new bed was, and stretched out on its thick mattress of straw and blankets.

Through tired eyes he gazed out across the lair. He could hardly believe it. Just a short while ago he had been talking to Tom on the corner of Merlin Place, and now he was hiding from a mysterious magician under a dark fortress with a bunch of grey kids with weird names. And what about Tom, where was he now?

It's all like some strange and terrible nightmare, Billy thought. *Though I'm sure I'm not as scared of the dark as I was before. There's no way I could have crept along creepy dark tunnels then, or sat all alone in the park at night.*

Billy could feel his confidence starting to grow. He was gradually getting stronger.

12

The next day, Billy lay on his bed in its nook in the wall, thinking. He was trying to come up with another escape plan and wondering if he was ever going to get back inside his house.

I could climb onto the roof and slide down inside the chimney, he thought, but then he had a vague memory that his dad had blocked the fireplace up last year.

OK, so maybe I could lift some of the roof tiles and jump down into the loft, he reasoned. *That might work!*

Suddenly Ace's head appeared in the

opening of the recess, interrupting his thoughts.

'Fancy going scavenging?' he asked, with a friendly grin. 'We need some new pots and pans.'

'Sure,' said Billy. His brain had become clogged with ideas that didn't go anywhere, and he was grateful for the chance to do something different.

'Stick close to me, and keep a sharp lookout for any creatures,' said Ace, handing Billy a scavenging sack.

'Not crawlers again – I hate them things,'

he said, immediately starting to panic. These creeping little men had always haunted his nightmares, but now they were haunting him for real.

'Don't worry, Billy, you don't get many in the fortress. Most of 'em are out patrolling the town,' said Ace. Then his narrow, freckled face turned pale and he grimaced. 'Anyway, it's the were'ounds we really need to worry about!' he said.

'Werehounds!' gasped Billy. 'You mean there are more creatures out there?'

'Loads, and they all have their job to do,' said Ace. 'The snufflers are like bloodhounds, tracking down escapees, and the collectors are the fortress gaolers. The crawlers patrol the town and the witches and warlocks do all the potion-making.'

'And the werehounds? What do they do?'

'Their speciality is ultra-violence. They're the fortress's special guards, and answer only to the Magician himself. They keep watch from the battlements, and if they catch a Runner they'll rip them to shreds in a second. They're my very worst nightmare, Billy. They make the crawlers seem like harmless little puppy dogs.'

With that cheery thought ringing in his ears, Billy followed Ace out of the lair and up into the fortress. He tried to memorize their route as they hurried along myriad gloomy lanes, but he soon become disorientated. The walls either side dripped with moisture and exuded a strong, bitter scent – it was the smell of fear and the whole fortress seemed steeped in it.

Eventually they came to a narrow courtyard, deep in shadow. Opposite stood the large, soot-blackened kitchen block.

'Be extra-careful now,' Ace warned, as they crept up to its heavy wooden door. 'The kitchen is the witches' special domain. If you're caught you'll end up as one of their ingredients!'

Billy blanched. 'Seriously?' he asked, his greying face turning ashen.

'Seriously,' said Ace solemnly. 'They wouldn't hesitate to chuck us in a blender and turn us into pâté. But don't worry, the morning meals have already been served an' the witches will be having their own breakfast by now.'

He eased open the kitchen door and slipped inside. A second later, he popped his head back out.

'Yeah, all clear,' he whispered.

Billy took a deep breath and nervously followed him in. A line of huge pots was bubbling and steaming away, and Billy recognized the smell of the intoxicating food he had eaten in the Bright Room. Even now it made him yearn to go back there.

On his left was a large blender, the inside coated with a thick grey paste, and Billy shuddered in horror. *Surely that's not a night-child turned to pâté*, he thought, feeling bile rise to his throat as he hurried past.

Along the far wall, a line of shelves was filled with bottles of strange, brightly coloured liquids and powders. More shelves sagged under the weight of sauces and herbs and plates of ham, beef, cheese and bread. Billy's head reeled with the wonderful aromas.

'Awesome,' he muttered, but Ace had scurried over to a door in the opposite wall. He put an ear to it, and then carefully and silently slid its heavy bolt closed.

'Come an' have a listen,' Ace whispered, beckoning him over.

Billy tiptoed across to join him. He could hear muffled voices coming from the other side. He raised his eyebrows questioningly, and Ace put a hand around his ear and whispered.

'It's the witches,' he said. 'Want to check 'em out?'

'Are you crazy?' gasped Billy. 'That's asking for trouble.'

'It'll be OK,' whispered Ace, and he began to climb a rickety staircase that led to another door, high up in the wall. 'Follow me.'

'You sure?' asked Billy.

'Yeah – nothing'll distract the witches once they've got their snouts in the trough.' Ace grinned.

So Billy reluctantly followed him up the stairs and through a door onto a wide landing. A terrible cackling noise filled the air and a dreadful smell stung his nostrils. He peered over the stone balustrade and looked down into a great hall. Two long rows of trestle tables ran down the centre of the room, and hunched over bowls of stew and grabbing at hunks of bread sat a gathering of dry, dusty, wrinkled witches and warlocks. They sounded like ravenous pigs at a trough, and the sight of them made Billy feel sick.

'You'll never guess what Drago told me,' Billy heard a witch say amongst the confusion of voices. 'That collector who let the night-child escape, they strung him up by his—'

Suddenly one of the hags smashed her fist onto the table. It was Morwella.

'Sshhilensh! Can you shmell shomething?' she cried. 'The shtench

of boy, perhapsh?'

Immediately, a hundred faces were lifted up and a hundred long twitching noses

sniffed the air. Billy and Ace ducked below the banister and peered between the pillars.

'I can smell something horrible,' said one witch, and the noses twitched again. Then there was a long, loud rasping noise, and somebody gave a cry of dismay.

'Phwar! It's you, Snaggletooth. That's disgusting!'

'Pardon me, I'm sure,' cackled Snaggletooth, an ancient, dumpy warlock who looked very pleased with himself, as amid a cacophony of complaints the others resumed their meal.

Ace tugged at Billy's sleeve.

'They'll be 'ere for a while yet. Let's get back to our scavenging,' he whispered, and Billy followed him back into the steaming kitchen.

'What do we need?' asked Billy, taking out his scavenging sack.

'Pans, spoons, knives and forks,' Ace replied, opening a drawer and tipping its contents into his own sack.

Billy took a frying pan and a cheese grater from under a bench, but his gaze kept being drawn to the delicious food weighing down the shelves. 'Can't we take some of that back too?' he asked as he started filling his sack.

'Sure,' Ace said and rolled a ladder on wheels along the shelves, and climbed right to the top. 'Catch!' he whispered, and started throwing down tins of peaches, evaporated milk and jars of pickle. Billy put those in his sack as well.

Cauldrons bubbled, ovens steamed and pipes hissed, and they were both so engrossed in their work they didn't hear the door from the courtyard creak open.

'Hey, Billy,' said Ace with a chuckle. 'What's smelly, ugly and bouncy?'

'I don't know,' replied Billy. 'What is smelly, ugly and bouncy?'

'A witch on a trampoline!' said Ace.

'Oh, very funny, I'm sure,' said a high, rasping voice and they turned to see a short podgy witch standing in the middle of the room with her hands on her hips. She looked as angry as an agitated wasps' nest. 'You're for the pot, you disgusting little squirts.'

'RUN!' cried Ace, and slid down the ladder as expertly as a fire fighter.

Billy scarpered, darting around cupboards and cookers as the witch tried to grab him, cackling all the while like a manic hyena.

'Give up, you little blighters. I've got you cornered!' she squealed in delight, but Billy feinted to the left, then right, and managed to weave past her.

'Too slow!' he cried, glancing back over his shoulder – and ran straight into a tall male

witch blocking the exit. It was Jasper, the warlock with the warty nose, and he grabbed Billy by the ear.

'I knew zat I would get you,' he cried. He bent down and pushed his face close to Billy's, staring at him with a bloodshot eye. Billy could smell his foul breath. 'I'll grind your bonezz to paste,' he hissed, and dug his pointed, witchy fingernails into Billy's earlobe.

'Yeeow!' Billy cried out in pain. Then he felt himself being lifted high into the air. He kicked and struggled, but the warlock was immensely strong and carried him over to the large blender. With a flick of his elbow, Jasper flipped up the lid and held Billy over the open cylinder. He could see the blender's enormous blades at the bottom start to spin.

'No!' yelled Billy. '*NO!*'

From the corner of his eye he saw Ace lower his shoulder and charge at the first witch, hitting her hard in the tummy.

'Oof!' gasped the crone, doubling over and gasping for breath. Ace grabbed a trolley laden with crockery, and gave it an almighty shove. It clattered across the floor and caught Jasper with a powerful, glancing blow on his bony hip.

'Arrgh!' he yelled, letting go of Billy and clutching his side in pain.

Billy landed across the opening of the whining machine. The blades whirled beneath him and he felt himself start to slip, but with all his strength he managed to pull himself up and with a sideways roll he dropped to the floor.

Now there came the sound of hurrying footsteps from the room next door.

'*Scarper!*' yelled Ace. Billy didn't need telling twice and bolted for the door.

'Come back, you vermin,' demanded the two witches, hobbling after them as a great pounding of fists erupted against the door to the witches' dining room. There came a thump, then another, and a splintering of wood as the doors caved in and the rest of the witches streamed into the kitchen from the great hall.

'COME BACK!' they screeched, but Billy and Ace were already out of the room and running for their lives across the courtyard. The grisly gang of hags followed hot on their heels, screaming like banshees.

Suddenly, somewhere close by, Billy heard a high jarring howl and juddered with fear.

'What's that?' he gasped.

'Trouble,' said Ace, and a look of sheer panic crossed his face. 'It's the were'ounds. If they get us, we'll be mincemeat.'

Billy ran full pelt, not daring to look to the left or right as screeches and growls echoed all around them. The noise rebounded from walls, so you couldn't tell where it was coming from. Billy was completely lost, but Ace seemed to know every dark alley, every shadowy short cut and deserted courtyard. Billy stuck to his heels, and soon he was squeezing along the secret tunnel that led to their lair.

'We made it!' he cried, as he staggered into the cave.

'Yee-ha!' crowed Ace, and the two boys burst out laughing with sheer relief.

13

The very next morning Billy was back in the streets between the teeming buildings of the fortress, stealing along alleyways as black as pitch. He had really wanted to go back to his house again, all on his own this time, and try out the idea he'd had to lift some of the roof tiles. If he found he could get inside, he could then go in search of Tom and they'd all be able to escape the dark world together.

But his plan had been put on hold. Instead, he was part of a deadly mission to rescue night-children from the Pits. He was struggling to remember everything Lightning had told him.

The evening before, she had gathered the Runners together and unrolled a large map across the table. It was made of hundreds of scraps of paper, all stuck together with tape and drawn by many different hands. It showed a plan of the fortress and the land beyond, and Billy whistled in amazement. He'd had no idea just how huge the fortress was.

As Lightning described the route they would take through the dark streets, then across a bleak moor and on to the dreaded Pits, Billy realized it would be fraught with danger.

'What on earth are the Pits?' he asked.

'Huge quarries where the rock to build the fortress is mined,' she replied. 'It's a dreadful place, Billy. The most petrified night-children are sent there. They're forced to dig out rocks with a pick and shovel, and the work is so hard and so relentless it breaks their spirit. Lots of them are desperate to escape. You will help, won't you?'

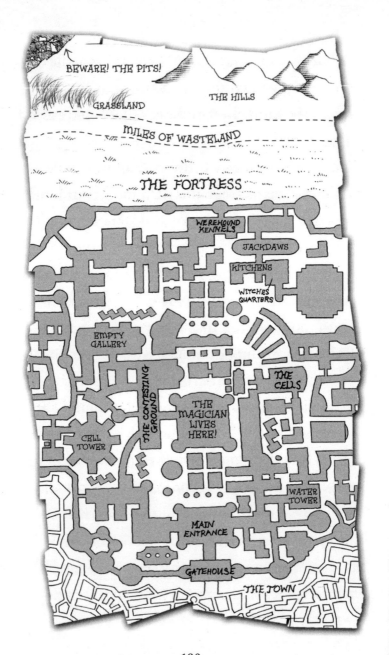

'Of course,' said Billy. The very thought of it made him nervous, but he knew he should repay the Runners' kindness. They had rescued him, after all.

Now, as they reached a rusted iron grille set in the castle's outer wall, a mournful howl rolled across the dark sky and Billy looked up to see a row of hunchbacked werehounds patrolling the battlements high above. It was the first time he had seen the Magician's elite guard, and even at that distance they made him catch his breath in horror.

He huddled in the shadows as Ace and Dusty lifted the grating clear, and propped it against the wall. Then he squeezed through the gap with the others and ran up a narrow road that bordered the open countryside beyond.

Billy recognized a five-barred gate with a rusty sign reading, 'KEEP OUT'. He passed this field with his mum and dad when they went to visit his grandparents, and the sudden memory made him realize how very much he missed them, and he was more determined than ever to get back home. He silently followed the Runners over the gate and into the field.

A blustery wind blew ragged clouds across the cold moon as Billy ran up the slope of the meadow and crossed into the next field. The distant cawing of jackdaws made him shudder, as he remembered the bird that had attacked him in his front room.

Soon the ground became coarser and lumpier, pitted with craters and covered with tall grasses that whipped against his legs. It took Billy a little while to realize they were crossing the site of the old brickworks outside town. He had been here a few times with Tom, and they'd had a great time riding their mountain bikes up and down the hollows.

Poor Tom. Where is he now? he wondered.

Finally, they reached the top of a high ridge,

and Billy crouched behind a rocky outcrop.

'Right, we're at the Pits,' said Lightning. 'Check it out.'

Eyes bright with fear, Billy looked over the rocks, and gaped in horrified wonder at the scene below.

Night-children were swarming across the pale walls of a vast crater, hacking away with pickaxes and sending great boulders crashing to the quarry floor. Other children, looking ragged and exhausted, split them into square blocks with mallets and wedges. Dust swirled around the quarry, and the sound of a thousand clinking tools filled the air.

It's the old limestone quarry, thought Billy to himself, though it didn't look much like the place he knew. It had been shut down years ago and turned into a nature reserve, but here it was a huge, livid scar of white rock that seemed to glow in the darkness. Then Billy saw something that made his heart nearly stop.

'What are . . . ?' was all he managed to croak before his voice dried.

'Shadowmen,' said Lightning. 'They guard the Pits workers, and they've filled my nightmares ever since I can remember.'

Billy had never seen anything like them. They were huge ominous smudges in the dark, as if they were clouds made of some foul dust, but they were gigantic, as tall as two men, and looked immensely strong. They were dotted around the quarry, shouting orders in deep bull-like bellows, and herding the frightened children around.

'Soon, some of the night-children will be escorted back to their cells,' Lightning told him. 'They go along the narrow pass below, and that's where we'll strike.'

Billy peered into the murky shadows, and could just make out a path running along the base of the ridge. It was an excellent place for an ambush.

'We'll slither down the embankment as silently as snakes, an' then, *wham*, they won't know what's hit 'em!' said Ace with a grin.

They settled down to wait. Time dragged by, and just as Billy was starting to think Lightning had got her timings wrong, he heard something. Above the clinking of tools came the thump of large feet, and he stared apprehensively into the pass below. At first he couldn't see a thing. Then a shadowman stepped into a patch of moonlight followed by a group of exhausted children. Another shadowman took up the rear.

Billy looked at Lightning. She was staring intently into the pass, a wild look in her eye. Then she raised her hand and waved it forward. The gang rose as one and crept over the ridge like a tribe of Sioux warriors. They split into two groups – one heading for the lead shadowman, one for the rear. Billy's heart was thundering and his nerves were as tense as wire, but he'd never felt more alive.

Following Lightning, he slid silently down the bank on his bottom, hunkered down behind some bushes and waited. As the shadowmen drew level, Lightning let out an ear-splitting yell.

'Chaaaarge!'

Billy leaped from his hiding place and ran straight towards the giant shadowmen, hollering at the top of his voice.

Taken by surprise, the shadowmen stopped in their tracks. One group of Runners headed for the guard at the rear, as Billy and his gang went for the first. They barged into its legs, hitting it just below the knee. Billy half expected to pass straight through it, but it wasn't made of shadow at all. It was like hitting a massive tangle of scratchy wool, and Billy's hands disappeared up to the wrists in the shadowman's prickly, dark matter.

The clumsy ogres bellowed loudly, staggered

backwards and tripped over the rest of the Runners, who had crouched down behind them. They hit the ground with a thump.

'We are the Runners – come and join us!' Billy heard Lightning yell amidst the pandemonium. Some of the night-children ran towards her, but others were too scared to move.

Billy grabbed a boy's hand and dragged him along in his wake. 'Come on, let's go!' he urged, but the boy's eyes were full of fear.

'W-w-what's happening?' he stammered, pulling his hand free. 'Who are you?'

'I'm Billy, a Runner, and we're rescuing you, so come on!' said Billy.

Still the boy seemed reluctant.

'We haven't got much time,' hissed Billy, pointing to one of the shadowmen as it began to sit up.

'O-O-O-K!' the night-child cried, and they took off.

As the moon appeared from behind a black cloud and lit up the pass, Billy glanced at the boy running beside him and did a double take! He was extremely thin with ears that stood out like wing nuts, and even though his eyes bulged and his skin was grey, Billy was sure he recognized him. Then the feeling was gone and Billy supposed he had imagined it.

A loud bellow shook the air, and Billy stopped in his tracks. He turned to see the shadowmen struggle to their feet and herd the remaining Pit workers into a tight group. Dusty was still amongst them! As he made a dash for it, a shadowman grabbed him by the scruff of the neck and drew him into a tight hug.

'Eeeaaargh!' the boy screamed.

'Dusty!' cried Billy, staring in horror as the shadowman squeezed tighter and tighter.

'Help me!' Dusty yelled, but the boy's cries were cut short as he disappeared into the mass of fuzzy darkness that was the ogre's body. Soon there was nothing left of him at all. Billy couldn't believe what he had just seen.

'Hurry up, Billy. There's nothing we can do,' Lightning shouted. Then a third shadowman came thumping along the pass towards them, its footsteps sounding like great sacks of flour smacking the ground.

Billy shook himself out of his trance and was off again, leading his rescued night-child up a narrow track that led to the ridge. The shadowmen were too slow and clumsy to tackle the steep climb, but they set up a loud and steady call.

'Right,' Lightning said, once Billy reached the top. 'Total silence from now on. Keep close and stay vigilant.'

Billy stood silent and shaking.

'Are you OK?' Lightning asked.

'Didn't you see? Dusty just disappeared!' he said.

Lightning nodded grimly. 'I know. It's awful, Billy, but we've got to carry on.'

'Is he . . .' Billy began, but couldn't finish the sentence.

'Dead? No, but I wouldn't want to be in his shoes,' said Lightning in a faltering voice. 'He's been absorbed into the shadowman's dark matter. He'll be reconstituted later, like instant mashed potato, and then he'll really be for it.' She looked towards the horizon. 'We should be moving on,' she said. 'OK?'

Billy was shocked to the core, but knew Lightning must have lost many friends to the demons of the night, and he mustn't hold

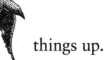

things up.

'Yeah, let's go,' he said, and off they went at a brisk pace, keeping to the hollows and sunken tracks that littered the ridge.

Everything was going well until they got halfway back to the fortress. Then, without warning, a huge flock of jackdaws dropped from the sky like dive-bombers.

'Watch out!' someone yelled, and the children scattered in all directions.

Billy took to his heels, leaping blindly over rocks and hurdling great tussocks of grass as

the birds screeched and pecked and clawed at his head. Eventually, and with a grateful sob, he all but fell into a deep, dry ditch and hid amongst the bracken. His face was crisscrossed with scratches and blood trickled from cuts to his hands as he lay motionless amongst the ferns, and the birds wheeled noisily overhead.

He waited a long time before he was sure they had gone, and then he parted the bracken and cautiously climbed from the ditch.

'Is that y-y-you, Billy?' came a voice from amongst the undergrowth, and Billy recognized it instantly. A head popped up from the bottom of the ditch. It was the boy he'd rescued – though it was the voice of his best friend that Billy had recognized.

'Tom!' said Billy.

'N-no, 5572,' the boy said, a little unsurely.

'Don't you know me?' asked Billy. His friend had changed even more since he'd seen him in the Bright Room, but he felt sure he could see the shadow of his face in the wide-eyed, grey-skinned night-child before him. 'We go to the same school – we're in the same class. *We're best mates!*'

The boy looked bewildered and shook his head. He looked like he had no idea what Billy was on about. 'I'm 5572,' he repeated.

Billy grabbed his hand and pulled him from the gully. 'Never mind,' he said. 'We'd better try and get back to the lair.'

They were atop a high, rock-strewn hill, and Billy's heart sank as he peered across the moonlit scene below. In the distance he could see the fortress, but there was no sign of the other Runners. All his fears of the dark came flooding back so fast they almost overwhelmed him, but he knew he had to be brave for Tom, or whoever this petrified night-child might be. He looked even more scared than Billy felt.

He took the watch from his pocket and felt its little ticking heartbeat. He remembered again what his dad had told him about how it could help, and blinked back his tears. He felt further away from home than ever, but holding the watch gave him strength.

'Come on,' he said, trying to sound brave.

The boy nodded nervously, and they scrambled down the hill together. A mile away the fortress stood like a great cliff, surrounded by the tumbledown houses of the town, and Billy set off towards it, keeping his eyes peeled for anything lurking in the dark, windswept countryside. The night-child was a bundle of nerves, jumping at the slightest sound, but Billy kept reassuring him and they made it back to the fortress's towering outer wall without incident.

'We should be OK now,' Billy said, helping his friend through the hole for the grating, and into one of the dark lanes that wound like a labyrinth between the fortress buildings.

But their troubles were far from over.

14

'Give us a hand,' whispered Billy, trying to lift the heavy grating back into place, but it slipped from his fingers and hit the ground with a *CLANG!*

A cacophony of howls erupted in the distance.

'That's torn it,' gasped Billy. 'Let's get outta here!'

They raced pell-mell down the lane, but as he careered around a corner Billy saw a distant posse of werehounds already loping towards them. He skidded to a halt. Ace was right – they were horrifying, like creatures summoned from the depths of the underworld.

As tall and broad as men, the hounds walked on their hind legs, snarling and snapping and lifting their heads to howl at the moon. They wore armoured breastplates and some carried sputtering torches in their front paws. Their jaws dripped with drool and their eyes glowed red in the flickering light.

Billy doubled back, pulling the night-child into the entrance of a narrow alleyway. His heart was thumping like a steamhammer.

'Come on – if they catch us, we'll be dog meat,' he said, but the boy was rooted to the spot.

'I'm not joking!' urged Billy. The night-child shook himself from his trance and Billy dragged him down the passage as excited howls erupted behind them.

'Whaaooooh!' The hounds were hot on their trail.

They raced into a small courtyard, and Billy cried out in horror. He had led them straight into a dead end! He pulled the boy into the deepest shadows as the werehounds appeared at the far end of the passage and prowled slowly towards them, their guttural growls getting closer and closer.

'We're d-d-done for, B-Billy,' whispered the night-child.

Then the clouds thinned slightly, and in the dim light of the moon, Billy saw rows of protruding bricks climbing in a decorative pattern up the courtyard walls. They were like flights of tiny steps.

'Not yet we're not. Follow me!' he said, and began to climb. They were only just wide enough to stand on and he had to flatten himself against the wall, feeling for fingerholds and hanging on for dear life. Angry snarls erupted in the courtyard below, and Billy forced himself to look down. The hounds were prowling around the yard, desperately searching for their prey.

'Please don't look up,' he *whispered* to himself, but they were lucky as the hounds had completely lost their scent. Frustrated and already worked into a frenzy, the animals started snapping amongst themselves. Then, with an explosion of barking and yelps of pain, they turned on each other, ripping great mouthfuls of fur from each other's pelts.

Billy's legs had turned to jelly but he continued to climb, guiding his petrified

companion all the way. When he reached a wide, unglazed window he climbed over the sill and lowered himself inside. He was in a large empty room, its shadowy corners swathed in spiders' webs that hung from the ceiling like dusty grey curtains.

'Billy!' came a small voice from outside, and he leaned out and pulled the night-child in after him.

'You OK?' Billy asked.

The boy nodded. His chest was heaving as he tried to catch his breath, and he slumped to the floor with exhaustion.

'Look, I can't call you by a number,' said Billy, sitting down beside him. '5572 sounds silly. I know your real name is Tom. Can't you remember anything about your home – don't you recognize me?'

The boy stared at Billy, his face creased in concentration. He shook his head.

'Please, think!' said Billy, who had forgotten for a moment that he had changed too. 'You're getting a new X-Station for your birthday and you invited me round to play. We go to Castle Lane School.'

Slowly, the boy's face started to clear. 'Wait a mo'. I think I d-do remember – but only bits. You've changed, Billy.'

'We all have,' said Billy.

Then a wide, beaming smile formed on Tom's face. 'Oh, yes! Now I r-r-remember. There's a teacher called, um, Mr . . . Grisly?'

'Near enough – it's old Grisly Griswald!' Billy laughed. Now he had found Tom, he didn't feel so alone and tears of joy welled up in his eyes. 'And don't worry, Tom,' he said, as the two friends grinned at each other in sheer delight. 'One day we're going to escape from this place and get back home.'

'How?'

'Well, I'm still working on that,' said Billy a little sheepishly, getting to his feet and brushing the dust from his hands. 'But we're not going to achieve anything sitting about here. First, we need to get back to the Runners' lair. You up to it?'

The boy nodded. 'W-w-which way do we go?'

'Good question!' said Billy, going over to the only door in the room. He turned the handle and gently pushed it open. The rusty hinges screeched loudly, but the corridor on the other side was deserted. 'I guess we'll have to go this way,' he said.

It was a long and gloomy passage, and the silence was overwhelming. They passed small rooms, sparsely furnished with cobweb-covered chairs, old mattresses and three-legged tables. Then Billy became aware of the shuffling of footsteps up ahead. Someone was coming the other way.

'Oh, brilliant!' he whispered sarcastically, and ducked into one of the side rooms. There was a table in one corner, with a jug of water and a mouldy truckle of cheese on it. Next to it stood a large chest, and he darted over and lifted the lid. It was full of old blankets.

'Quick, in here!' hissed Billy.

The footsteps were getting closer, and with a look of sheer panic Tom leaped in. Billy clambered in after him, covering them both with blankets. He'd only just closed the lid when the shuffling feet entered the room.

Billy peered through a crack in the wood, trying to make out who their visitors were. He could see a mess of purple hair, the back of a wrinkled bald head, two black cloaks and some long pointed fingers.

'A witch and a warlock!' whispered Billy.

'Oh, I hate witches,' whimpered Tom, his voice only half-muffled by the blankets. 'They give me terrible nightmares.'

'Sshh,' warned Billy, but he could feel Tom's whole body shivering with fear.

Then there was a cracking of arthritic bones and the chest creaked as somebody sat on it. Billy heard a man's voice, his congested nose making him breathe heavily through his mouth, so he sounded like a blocked drain. Billy was sure he recognized it, but he couldn't remember where from.

'I've had enough of looking after this flamin' prisoner,' the warlock complained. 'Let's do away with her, once and for all.'

'And defy the Magician? You must be out of your tiny mind,' a woman's voice croaked. 'Come on, it's time she was fed.'

The man gave a growl of frustration. 'I'd like to snap her stupid neck,' he hissed, but the chest moved as he got to his feet. Then there was a crash and the sound of breaking glass.

'Now look what you've done!' snapped the woman. 'Get a cloth and wipe it up.'

'Don't squawk so,' said the man, and then, to Billy's horror, the lid of the chest was opened and the top blanket was whipped away. He was staring straight up at the bald warlock, and he recognized him instantly – it was the creepy old man who'd served him in the convenience store!

Luckily he was glowering across at his companion, but all he had to do was turn his head and he would see the boys amongst the

blankets. Then it would all be over, and Billy and Tom would find themselves back in their cells. Billy didn't dare breathe, and he squeezed Tom's shaking hand for reassurance. This could be it!

The warlock's knees cracked like gunshots as he knelt down and mopped up the spill on the floor. Then, swearing and growling, he got to his feet, grabbing the edge of the chest to steady himself. His fingers almost brushed the end of Billy's nose. They smelled of something rotten and Billy nearly gagged. Finally the wrinkled warlock threw the soggy blanket back in the box and slammed the lid shut without looking down once.

'Come on,' the woman croaked, and Billy heard them shuffle out of the room. He let out a huge sigh of relief, flipped back the lid and tumbled out of the chest. Tom climbed out after him.

'Have they g-g-gone?' he asked in a tremulous voice.

'Yeah, all clear,' said Billy, peering around the door. 'C'mon, let's follow them and find out who their prisoner is.'

'Are you crazy?' cried Tom. 'I hate w-w-witches, Billy.'

'But the prisoner might be another night-child,' said Billy. 'We might be able to help her.'

Tom remained silent, staring at the ground, and Billy could tell he was seriously scared.

'OK, it's no problem. I can always return later with some of the Runners,' he said. 'Let's get back to the lair.'

'N-n-no, you're right, Billy,' murmured Tom. 'We should at least find out who the prisoner is.'

'You sure? You really don't have to.'

'Y-y-yeah – I was just being a w-w-wimp,' said Tom, flushing a darker shade of grey.

'No worries. We're all scared of something,' said Billy, feeling braver than he had for a long time, and putting a reassuring arm around his friend's shoulders.

15

'Gross!' complained Billy, as they followed the sour odour of the ancient witches along the corridor. 'There's no mistaking which way they went!'

Eventually, they came to a large room. In the centre was a stone-built cell with a thick solid door. A barred window was set into each side.

'Wake up, you wretch,' screamed the warlock, clattering a stick along the bars.

Billy crept into the room after them, hiding behind a pillar at the side of the entrance and beckoning Tom to follow. The purple-haired witch opened a hatch at the bottom of the cell door, and Billy heard a shuffling noise coming from inside.

'Here's your food!' croaked the witch, and kicked a plate of mouldy bread and cheese through the gap.

'If it was up to me, we'd be feeding you to the werehounds,' spat the bald warlock through his slack, wet lips, as he peered through the bars with a beady, bloodshot eye.

'Well it's not up to you, so clear off. Hee-hee!' answered a small voice.

'Just you wait. My chance will come, and then you won't be so cocky!' he said in his thick, snotty whine. 'See you later.'

'Get lost!' said the voice.

The witches gave each other a ghastly grin and shuffled out of the room. As soon as they had gone Billy hurried over to the cell, climbed onto a bunker below one of the windows and peered through the bars. A small hooded figure sat at a table with its back towards him.

'It's a night-child!' whispered Billy, as Tom climbed up beside him. 'Hey, you – pssst!'

The figure jumped at the sound of his voice and turned to face them. Billy gasped in surprise – she was a night-child all right, no taller than Billy himself, but her grey skin was as puckered as a shrivelled potato. She looked like a little old woman who had never grown up!

'Are you OK?' said Billy, somewhat taken aback. 'Who are you?'

'Fleetfoot,' said the strange night-person.

I've heard that name before, thought Billy, as she jumped from the stool and hurried over to the barred window. She climbed onto the bed so her face was level with his, and squinted at him with eyes that had turned milky with age.

'You're Runners!' she exclaimed.

'That's right. I'm Billy, and this is Tom.'

Tom gave her a nervous little wave.

'I'm a Runner too, ha-ha!' giggled Fleetfoot, then looking over each shoulder, as if to double-check there was no one else around, she added in a whisper, 'I knew someone would come eventually – hee-hee. It's true you know, Billy. It's all true.'

'What is?' asked Billy, wondering how long she had been locked up on her own, and if she might have become a little unhinged.

'The sword!' said Fleetfoot, and she gave another high-pitched giggle.

Then it suddenly dawned on Billy. This was the Runner who had disappeared – the Runner who had gone looking for a mythical weapon that could defeat the mighty Magician. What was she doing locked up all on her own? Where were all her friends?

'When I was young, many years ago, I

used to go out scavenging – not for food, but for knowledge,' she said in a breathless rush. 'I'd sneak into the library where the fortress archives are kept, choose something interesting and climb to the highest beam in the ceiling. There I'd sit reading, way above the witchy librarian. I learned a lot about the fortress and how it works – and that's where I read about the sword.'

'What did you read?' asked Billy, starting to think she must be completely doolally.

With a grin, Fleetfoot took off one of her shoes, lifted the lining and removed a flattened and somewhat smelly roll of yellowed paper. She handed it to Billy.

'What do you think of that that?' she giggled.

Dubiously, Billy unfolded the paper and began to read out loud:

I write this note in the sure knowledge that I will not live beyond the hour. I am the last of an ancient order of Knights sworn to fight darkness in all its forms, and we have been on the trail of the Magician for an eternity. At my side hung the sword of brilliant light, the only weapon capable of destroying the Magician and his entire world. It is the one thing he is truly scared of.

    I discovered the location of his great fortress and, full of righteous confidence, I crept through its dark streets and climbed to the battlements. Here I was met by a pack of hounds as gruesome as nightmares. They came at me howling and slavering, and I chopped at their skeletal jaws, laying them senseless at my feet. But my great age began to tell and by the time I had despatched my last attacker I was fighting for breath. That is when the Magician himself appeared, and I saw his surprise and fear at the sight of the dazzling sword.

'By all that is good and noble, you are finished!' I cried, and raised the sword above my head. But as I stepped forward, I am ashamed to say that I stumbled and sank to my knees, all my strength gone. The Magician easily knocked the sword from my weak grasp.

'You have failed, Knight, and your life is forfeit,' he sneered. 'Have you any last request before I take it from you?'

'Allow me to leave a record of these last moments to mark the end of my order and our eternal quest, and record that you have won.' I said. He acceded to my wishes, and these few words mark the end of my lifetime search for the terrible Magician.

'Wow!' said Billy, astonished. 'That's amazing, but I don't know how it helps us.'

'Turn it over. There's more,' said Fleetfoot. 'And it's written by the Magician himself!'

Billy turned the sheet over, and scrawled across the back he read:

> All my worries are behind me, all danger past, and now I need fear nothing. The pompous knight has been dealt with, and at last I possess the dazzling sword.
>
> Its blinding light burned my skin, so I smashed it on the ground. Something broke off and the sword dimmed. Now my enemies will never be able to use it against me. Darkness is assured, and my supremacy unassailable.
>
> **M**

Billy gave a low whistle. 'But how do you know it's real, and isn't just part of some forgotten fable?'

'Because I found the sword, Billy,' said Fleetfoot. 'A weapon so powerful it can defeat the Magician! It took me years of searching, but I found it. Ha-ha!'

16

Billy's eyes darted around the cell, as if he expected to see the mighty sword propped up in a corner.

'So, where is it?' he asked.

'Oh, I haven't got it!' said Fleetfoot matter-of-factly. 'But I found a great block of stone with a sword carved on it. Then I got caught and the Magician locked me in here, far away from everyone else because I know where the sword is hidden.'

'Just a minute, you didn't actually see the sword. You just saw a carving!' said Billy incredulously. 'So how do you know it exists?'

'I could feel its power, Billy. It was so close it made my whole body tingle. I'm sure it's inside the stone! Now you boys must find it; find it and use it to defeat the Magician.'

'Whoa! Hold on a minute,' cried Billy. 'We're only twelve! We can't defeat a powerful magician.'

'N-n-no way,' stuttered Tom.

'Don't be so defeatist, Billy,' said Fleetfoot. 'Just think – if you can get the sword, you might free us all.'

'Yeah, but . . . it's the Magician!' said Billy, his voice taut with fear. He hadn't even seen the Magician properly, but his heart was beating nineteen to the dozen at just the thought of him.

'We're all scared, Billy, but someone has got to be brave enough to make a stand or we'll be stuck here for ever, hee-hee!'

'And actually, you really are very brave, Billy,' Tom butted in helpfully. Then, turning to Fleetfoot he said, 'He rescued me from the shadowmen, and he can remember his home and everything.'

'You can remember your home?' asked Fleetfoot, astonished.

'Well, yeah, but . . .' mumbled Billy.

'Well, that proves you're special, don't you see?' cried Fleetfoot. 'It means you're stronger than us – you can resist the Magician's magic. You must find the sword.'

'I don't know,' said Billy, feeling a bit daft.

'It's true,' said Fleetfoot. 'You could save us all.'

She might be as batty as a church tower, but Billy was starting to feel Fleetfoot could be right. He was forgetting more and more every day, and he knew that time was running out. But he was the only night-child who remembered their real home, and that might mean he was the only one who could get everyone back there. Defeating the Magician might be the only way any of them would ever get home. But was he really brave enough to stand up to the terrifying sorcerer?

He gripped his pocket watch. It was pulsing with an energy that seeped up his arm, across his chest and through his whole body, giving him a newfound courage. He knew now that the watch was exactly the good-luck talisman his dad had said it was.

'OK. So, where do I find this sword?' he asked.

'Hee-hee! I knew you'd help,' cried Fleetfoot. She jumped down from her bed, took the knife from her breakfast plate and cut a few threads along the seam of her mattress. Putting a long finger inside, she pulled out another crumpled piece of paper. It was a sketch of the main Keep of the fortress.

The top floor was labelled 'Magician's Quarters', the floor below 'Magician's Personal Guard', and below that was a section of blank

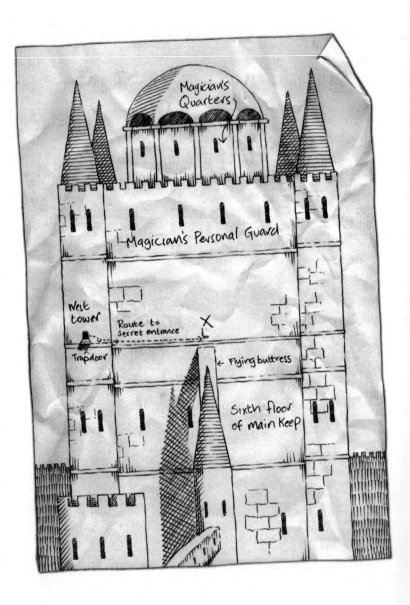

wall showing a hidden entrance marked with an X.

'That's where you must go – through the trapdoor, then along this ledge and behind a hidden slab in the wall,' said Fleetfoot.

'But that's where the Magician lives,' said Billy, with a shudder of fear. 'It'll be like going into the lion's den!'

Fleetfoot nodded. 'I never said it would be easy, Billy.'

'Have you got a map of the inside?'

'That would be impossible. You see, once you're in there, *nothing* makes sense at all!'

Billy was about to ask more questions when they heard shuffling footsteps coming along the passage. The witchy guards were returning.

'Go!' said Fleetfoot in a hoarse whisper.

'But we want to get you out of here,' said Billy.

'There's no time, but don't worry, Billy, you

can set us all free! Now, go. Vamoose!'

He and Tom dived behind the columns, just as the witches marched into the room.

'We 'eard you,' they rasped. 'Who were you talking to?'

'Myself, nitwits,' giggled Fleetfoot. 'Or did you think a couple of Runners had come to rescue me? Ha-ha-ha!'

'Move aside. We're going to check your cell.'

As the witches unlocked Fleetfoot's door, Billy and Tom hurried back to the room with the unglazed window and leaned out. The werehounds had gone from the courtyard below, and over to his left Billy could see the great central Keep where the Magician lived. Somewhere in there might be a weapon that could free them all.

'What d-d-do you think, Billy?' asked Tom. 'Did you believe all that stuff about a sword of light?'

'I'm not sure, but there's only one way to find out,' said Billy, climbing onto the window ledge. 'I'm going to try and find it.'

'Shouldn't you tell the other Runners f-f-first?'

'No. We can't all go trooping through the Keep. This is down to me. I'll show you the way back to the lair first, though.'

'N-n-no way, Billy. I'm not going to let you go on your own. And no arguments – you're my p-p-pal!' said Tom.

'Thanks, Tom,' said Billy. He felt a new confidence growing in him and was determined he would find the sword. 'Come on, let's go!'

A fuzzy shadowman waited patiently in a dim room, high up in the Keep. A black fog drifted silently in through the door.

It began to spin around the shadowman, getting faster and faster until it roared like a tornado. With a tearing sound, as if someone were pulling apart a huge sheet of Velcro, a figure was gradually, painfully, drawn from the shadowman's matter. It was pulled and stretched until, with a loud yell, it dropped to the floor. It was Dusty!

The fog solidified into the towering figure of the Magician, who studied the boy from beneath hooded eyes and smiled.

'Well, well, well, if it isn't a snivelling Runner,' said the Magician with a sneer. 'I've had enough of you and your friends. You are nothing but pests, irritants that should be stamped out. So, tell me where your hideout is, child, or it will be the worse for you.'

'Get lost!' said Dusty, though he was shivering with fear. He wasn't going to give his friends up.

'Oh dear. You foolish boy,' said the Magician, rolling his sleeves up as his hands started to spit dark fizzing sparks. 'I *demand* that you tell me where your hideout is!'

A storm of powerful magic whipped around Dusty's head and he became so scared he burst into tears and told the Magician everything.

Then, as a tearful Dusty was escorted back to a cell, the Magician melted into the shadows once more and drifted out of the room. He was headed to where the ancient prisoner, Fleetfoot, was kept. The witches had sent word they'd heard her talking to someone, and the Magician was determined to find out what was going on.

Of all his prisoners, she was the one he guarded most carefully, for she knew about the sword and where to find it. Yes, he could have easily disposed of her, but he would not give up the fear of even one of his night-children. Without their fear, he would be nothing and his kingdom would crumble. He needed every single one of them alive ... and afraid.

17

Billy edged his way along the base of the Keep until he reached the west tower. A strong wind was blowing, and a heavy blanket of cloud made the night seem darker than ever. Now he was up close to the Magician's quarters he wasn't sure it was such a good idea, but he was determined to go through with his plan. It might be his only chance of ever getting home.

'How do we g-get in?' Tom asked in a nervous whisper.

Billy shrugged. 'No idea,' he said.

He carried on around the tower, almost

missing a low metal door in the darkness. It felt rusty and warped out of shape. He gave it a shove, and it opened with a squeak.

'I don't believe it,' he whispered, pushing the door some more. 'It's not even locked!'

He stepped inside and there was a loud scrabbling as a swarm of rats ran for cover. A burning torch cast a trembling light across a litter-strewn floor and revealed a spiral staircase curving up into the gloom. Billy took the torch from its bracket, and with a nervous grimace towards his friend, he began to climb. Tom followed close on his heels.

The higher they climbed, the nearer they got to the Magician's private rooms, and Billy felt the air crackle with a terrible power. It made his skin prickle, as if a thousand ants were crawling over him, but he swallowed his fear with a gulp, took out Fleetfoot's sketch and studied it in the light of the torch.

'Only one more flight and we should find

the door through the wall,' he whispered. He was finding it harder to breathe now, as if some great weight was pressing down on his chest. When they reached the next landing he scanned the stonework, looking for a hatchway, but couldn't see any sign of one.

'It's got to be here somewhere,' he said, starting to worry. Maybe Fleetfoot had been crazy, after all.

'I c-c-can't see anything,' said Tom, peering over his shoulder.

Billy circled the inside of the tower, brushing aside cobwebs and moss. Just as he was about to give up, he uncovered a narrow slot in the mortar, like a letter box. He put his hand inside and felt a metal chain.

'This must be it!' he exclaimed. He grabbed the chain and tugged hard.

There was a dull clunk, and with a grinding noise a stone door slowly opened in the wall.

'Yes!' exclaimed Billy, his eyes shining with nervous excitement. He leaned out – it was a sheer and dizzying drop to the cobbled lanes below, but to his left was a narrow ledge running around the Keep, just as Fleetfoot had described. He propped the torch against the wall.

'OK?' he asked Tom. 'You've still got time to pull out.'

'N-n-n-no, I'm with you,' said Tom, though

he looked as nervous as Billy felt.

Billy climbed up into the opening and stepped out onto the ledge. It was windy and a heavy downpour had made the stone slippery. Not daring to look down, he edged slowly along until he came to a large slab standing slightly proud of the Keep's wall.

'This must be the secret entrance,' he shouted above the wind.

Tom nodded, too scared to speak.

Billy gave the slab a push and it sprang forward on stone runners. He climbed inside and helped his friend in after him.

'Thanks,' the boy gasped, with a sigh of relief. Then the slab closed silently behind them, and everything went black.

'Oh, brilliant,' whispered Billy sarcastically. He couldn't even see his hand in front of his face. Then a faint yellow glow appeared in the darkness.

'W-w-what's that?'

The light started to grow and spread. After so long in the dark it was painful to look at, and Billy had to shield his eyes. But, gradually, he became used to the glare and with a gasp of astonishment saw a wide landscape of rolling fields spread out before him. It seemed to go on for miles, all the way to a distant horizon

and a clear, golden sky. A small river sparkled as it wound its way before a dense wood, and the air was full of birdsong.

'Oh, w-w-wow! It's amazing,' cried Tom.

'Incredible,' said Billy, basking in the warmth of the sun. It felt so good after the gloom and damp of the fortress he really wanted to lie down and soak up the golden rays for ever. But the air tingled with magic, like the air in the Bright Room, and he knew it must be an illusion and that they were still inside the Keep.

'Come on, we have to move on,' he said, realizing they would have to fight against the Magician's magic all the way.

'But w-w-where do we go?' asked Tom.

'Good question,' said Billy, but as he spoke he heard a faint rumble in the distance and a thin, jagged mountain began to rise between two conical hills on the horizon. It was shaped like a crooked finger. 'That's got to be the way,' he said excitedly. 'Look! It's beckoning us on!' Perhaps it was a trick of the light, but the finger of rock seemed to be moving.

'I d-don't like it,' said Tom, his large eyes growing even wider. 'It might be a t-t-trap.'

'Maybe, but I don't know where else to go,' said Billy, and they set off down the grassy knoll towards the mountain. The sun was shining, the air was fresh and clear and everything seemed perfectly normal. And then, in an instant, it all changed.

The ground beneath his feet turned soft and spongy, like marshmallow.

'What's going on?' Billy shouted. He was sinking into the ground, and the more he struggled the deeper he sank. Soon he was up to his knees in gluey, clinging mud. Tom was sinking too.

'It was a trap!' Tom cried. 'Help!'

'Over here!' yelled Billy. There was a wide slab of rock protruding from the ground, and he managed to pull himself onto it. Tom struggled towards him, but he was sinking ever deeper. Then the air began to congeal. It became as thick as syrup and they could only move in slow motion. It was like a bad dream.

'*Heeelp, B-B-Billeee!*' cried Tom, his voice drawling like a slowed-down recording as he sank up to his waist.

'*Don't paaanic!*' Billy hollered, but the

ground bubbled and popped and Tom sank up to his chest.

Without thought for his own safety, Billy slid back into the treacherous mire. He immediately started to sink, but grabbed hold of the edge of the slab to steady himself. Then he reached out with his other hand for Tom and started to pull with all his might. He pulled so hard he thought he might break in two, but inch by inch he managed to drag Tom towards him. Eventually, his friend was close enough to grab hold of the rock.

Billy had sunk up to his waist, but with a monumental effort he turned round in the viscous mud and dragged himself back onto the slab. He staggered to his feet, took Tom's hands and pulled his friend up beside him. As he did so, the air thinned and they could move normally again.

'Thanks, Billy,' said Tom in an exhausted whisper.

Billy nodded and collapsed back on the rock, taking in great gulps of air. As his rasping breathing subsided, he became aware of another noise – a loud rushing roar.

'What's that?' he asked, and sitting up gave a cry of surprise. The soft, sticky ground had turned to liquid and now a vast stormy ocean surrounded them. 'Watch out!' he shouted, as a strong swell washed across the rocks, swept him into the torrent and carried him out to sea.

Billy struggled to stay afloat as the swell

grew into a wave, and grew and grew again, lifting him up onto its foaming crest. His stomach flipped over and over, as if he were riding a giant roller coaster.

'Tom!' he cried, desperately looking for his friend as the towering wave carried him forward like a powerful juggernaut, high in the air. Then it pounded him down, and he sank deep below the waves. All he could see was green foaming water and his chest began to burn from lack of oxygen. Summoning all his strength he swam upwards, against the swirling current that was trying to force him down. With a rasping gasp, he broke the choppy surface and looked for his friend.

Tom had already worked a hard shift in the Pits before being rescued, and was floundering helplessly nearby. Billy grabbed him under the arms and headed for the distant shore. He could feel his own strength gradually ebbing away, but he wasn't going to abandon his best friend, and Billy finally pulled him onto a golden sandy beach.

'You saved me again,' spluttered Tom.

'No problem,' panted Billy, watching as the vast sea sank back into the ground, as if it was a huge sponge. Somehow Billy's clothes became instantly dry, and he knew for certain he was inside an illusion. But each challenge was making him more exhausted than the last.

'Look where we've landed!' he said, with relief. About a mile away, the great black mountain rose like a giant shard of jet amongst a line of gentle, sugarloaf hills.

The Magician was pleased with himself. He had gleaned all the information he needed from Dusty and Fleetfoot, and sent a team of crawlers to the Runners' lair. He had given the crawlers strict orders to drag the Runners from their beds and take them back to the tower of cells so that once again he could feed on their fear.

Now he sat with his eyes closed, waiting for news. Eventually, there was a timid knock at the door.

'Enter.'

A crawler slithered into the room.

'Is it done?' asked the Magician. 'Did you

get them all? Did they squeal and cry with fear?'

'Sssll, hisssss, slup,' dribbled his familiar.

'Good,' said the Magician, and his pale skin sparked as a wave of new energy swept through him. 'Now listen, and listen well. Tell the collectors to gather everyone together – and I mean everyone – and take them to the contesting ground and wait for me there. 5126 is going to be taught a lesson they will never, ever forget. No one will ever defy me again, and there will be no more Runners, once and for all!'

The crawler sniggered, spraying mucus from its snout, and scurried from the room.

Wrapping his cloak around him with a flourish, the Magician dispersed into a dark fog and sank through the floorboards.

18

Billy stood before the great curved finger of a mountain. A path led straight into a dark cave at its centre, and a cold wind blew from its gaping mouth.

'Don't tell me we've got to g-g-go inside the mountain,' said Tom, his grey face pale and tense. 'I still think it's a trap.'

'Me too, but if we want to find the sword we'll have to carry on,' said Billy with an uneasy grin. 'Wait there a minute.'

He walked cautiously up to the entrance and, after a moment's hesitation, stepped inside. A low humming noise emanated from

the rock, and a flash of light snaked around the cave's mouth. Billy waited, expecting something to happen, but the flashing died away and everything became silent.

'Come on, it's all right,' said Billy with a sigh of relief. But when his friend tried to follow, he couldn't. A wall of transparent rock had formed across the entrance, and Billy watched helplessly as Tom hammered on it with his fists – he was shouting something, but Billy couldn't hear a word he said. Then a werehound appeared out of nowhere and slunk towards the petrified boy.

'Watch out!' Billy screamed, but his friend couldn't hear and the hound grabbed him from behind. The glassy wall began to turn black and Tom gradually faded from view, wriggling and floundering in the hound's paws.

'Tom!' Billy yelled again, but he was gone and Billy was trapped inside the mountain. His knees buckled beneath him and he sank to the floor feeling marooned and alone, and horribly guilty about Tom – he should never have let him come on such a dangerous mission. Tears began to trickle down his face, but a gentle buzzing from his pocket watch reminded him of his quest, and he forcefully wiped his cheeks dry.

'You mustn't give up now. You mustn't,' he told himself firmly, getting to his feet.

Although it was dark inside the cave, somehow he could see quite clearly. It was like the inside of a great black cathedral that stretched back into the mountain. The walls were flanked with fluted columns of rock that soared up to a high vaulted ceiling, and at the far end of the cave, sitting in a beam of light, was a massive block of stone. It looked like a great tomb from a Victorian graveyard, and the vibrations from Billy's watch became more urgent.

'That's got to be the stone Fleetfoot was on

about!' he muttered, and hurried towards it, feeling small and vulnerable in the cave's vast silence. A sudden swishing noise stopped him in his tracks. He thought he saw a swirl of dark mist from the corner of his eye, and spun round. He could see all the way along the cave in both directions, but there was nothing there.

'Just my imagination,' he told himself, his heart hammering in his chest, and carried on.

The stone block was huge, a good head higher than Billy, with a great slab of polished

granite on top. Trembling with nervous excitement he climbed onto it. There, carved into its surface, was the image of a sword just as Fleetfoot had described. Billy felt sure the real sword was hidden inside too, for the air around it felt alive with energy, making his pocket watch rattle like an alarm clock.

He studied the granite slab, looking for a catch or keyhole. Surely there had to be a way to open the stone tomb – but how? Then he noticed a small carving of a fiery sun, just below the image of the sword. It was raised, like a button, and he pressed it with his thumb. It was set solid, and didn't move.

'NO!' Billy cried out loud. Had he come all this way for nothing? In sheer frustration, he stamped down on the stone orb with all his weight. There was a loud *click*, a hatch silently opened down the slab's centre and there, lying in a shallow cavity, was the legendary sword!

'WOW!' he gasped.

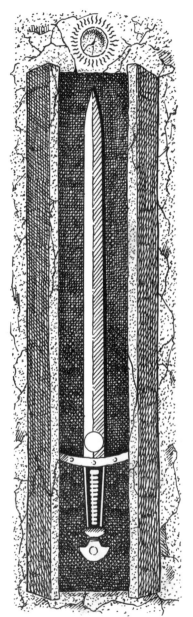

It was longer than Billy himself and made of a dull grey metal that pulsed slowly with a dim light. The handle was inset with a golden sun motif and deep blue lapis lazuli. It looked just like the engraving on the back of Billy's watch, and he knew they had to be connected. With a rush of excitement he squatted down and wrapped his hand around the sword's thick handle.

'Found what you were looking for?' asked a silky voice.

Billy spun round and gave a strangled gasp. Standing behind him was the terrifying figure of the Magician. He was over three metres tall, as thin as a whip and dressed in black

from head to toe. His face was as white as paper with a short snub nose and long, greasy beard. His coal-black eyes stared out from deep, dark sockets.

Billy was so shocked he just stood there, dumb with fear.

'Well, there's the sword – pick it up and try your luck,' said the cadaverous Magician in little more than a whisper. When Billy didn't move, he exploded with fury. 'Pick up the sword,' he bellowed, the stringy tendons in his neck standing out like cables.

Petrified, Billy grabbed the sword, determined to put up a fight. He lifted it a few centimetres and tried to swing it over his head. It was so heavy he toppled backwards off the slab and sprawled on the ground, the sword landing next to him with a resounding clang. He stared up at the Magician, his eyes wide with terror.

'How has a worm like you resisted my

magic?' sneered the Magician derisively. 'Well, my shivering little night-child, that is about to change.'

He swept his arm in a wide arc, and Billy gasped as the cave began to streak and melt away around him, like a painting left out in the rain. He found himself standing on a vast flat roof, high above the fortress courtyards. A low wall ran around the perimeter, next to which hundreds of cowering night-children had been gathered. They were packed onto the adjacent rooftops too, all guarded by collectors and crawlers, werehounds and shadowmen, who stared in rapture at the towering figure of their master.

'Just who are you?' Billy asked in a small and frightened voice.

The Magician leaned down and thrust his paper-white face into Billy's. 'I am your worst nightmare, boy,' he hissed. 'I am everybody's worst nightmare.'

Then the Magician drew himself up to his full height and extended his arms.

'I am the thump in the night that sets your heart pounding, and the scratch-scratch-scratching of night demons at your window pane,' he roared, and his words echoed around the sky. 'I am the fat, hairy spider that crawls out of your dreams and over your face, and the bloated serpent that slithers from beneath your bed to swallow you as you sleep. I am the night itself – I am your fear, 5126!'

Billy shook with terror. There was no chance he could defeat the Magician now. He'd failed.

19

The atmosphere felt charged with electricity and, unable to contain themselves, the watch creatures began to howl and whoop as they waited for the showdown to begin. Their cacophonous din filled Billy's head, making it difficult to think.

As the noise and excitement reached fever pitch, the Magician raised a hand and the creatures fell silent.

'Bring them here,' he said, and a werehound herded a small group of night-children towards them. Billy started – it was his friends, the Runners. They had been caught too. And then one of the werehounds loped forward and dropped Tom – ashen-faced – on the ground.

The Magician began to circle Billy, like a stalking tiger.

'Take a good look at your friend,' he said to the Runners with a sneer. 'Behold the pathetic whelp who thought he could save you.'

The Runners didn't say anything, but simply stared at Billy with wide, petrified eyes. He felt helpless and humiliated.

'He thought he was going to save you all,' shouted the Magician, sweeping his arm towards the crowds of night-children lining the perimeter wall. 'He told you he remembers another home, but that is not possible – *this* is his home. He said he has a name other than the number I gave him.'

The Magician bent down and put his face close to Billy's. His breath felt cold, like the air from a damp cellar, and smelled of rotting leaves. It made Billy's skin crawl.

'So, what is this special name, boy?' he scoffed.

Billy was too scared to speak. He looked to his friends for help. Lightning stared back full of hope, but Billy's mind felt completely blank.

'Tell us your name,' the Magician screamed, and suddenly all Billy could think of was a series of numbers.

'I am 5126!' he cried.

'Again. We didn't hear you,' the Magician yelled triumphantly.

'I am 5126,' Billy sobbed out loud, feeling utterly defeated. 'My name is 5126!'

20

The Magician snapped his fingers and a werehound backed out from a rooftop doorway, dragging the sword behind him. It was so heavy he had trouble lifting it, and he laid it at Billy's feet with a heavy clunk. Billy heard the Runners' gasp – they must have realized the sword they'd read about in the old journal really did exist.

'This is the miraculous weapon that legend says can destroy me. *Me*, the creator of this whole world, defeated by a rusty length of iron!' The Magician roared, his power growing ever stronger as waves of fear radiated from the crowds of night-children. 'Well, pick up the sword again, 5126. Pick it up and do your worst!'

Shamed in front of his friends, Billy stared at the ground, wishing it would swallow him up. He knew he had let them down. All his hopes of getting home were gone and his belief that he could destroy the Magician shown up as false arrogance. The memories of his mum and dad's faces were now no more than a faint blur.

But his watch had become hot in his pocket again – hot enough to burn his thigh. He knew it was important, but in his petrified state he couldn't remember why. Then as he stared at the sword on the ground, he noticed the shallow depression below its hilt.

From the depths of his confused mind, Billy remembered what he'd read in the Magician's note. How he had smashed the sword on the ground and something had broken off that gave the weapon its energy. Suddenly, and with complete clarity, he knew how they were connected.

In the secrecy of his pocket, Billy popped the engraved back off the watch. He knelt down and pushed it into the recess on the sword's blade. It fitted perfectly, and as it clicked into place the sword began to glow with a pure and intense light and Billy lifted it up as easily as a feather.

'Brilliant!' cried Ace from amongst the group of Runners, and the crowd of night-children murmured and jostled nervously.

'No!' the Magician croaked weakly. 'Where did you get that?'

Suddenly Billy could remember *everything*, as clear as day – his dad had given him the watch for protection, and as soon as he remembered that, everything else came rushing back to him. He felt a confidence and bravery he'd never experienced before.

'My name is Billy Jones and I don't belong here,' he said, swirling the weapon in the air like a master swordsman.

The Magician roared in fury.

'Yes, your name's Billy!' shouted Lightning.

'Go on, Billy, you can do it,' cried Tom.

Some of the Runners started to chant, quietly at first, and then louder and louder: 'Billy, Billy, Billy.'

'Silence!' screamed the Magician, and although his familiars growled and snapped, the rest of the night-children began to join in.

'BILLY, BILLY, BILLY!'

FIZZ! The Magician suddenly launched an attack and the chanting stopped. He sent a ball of electricity whipping through the air, but without having to think Billy parried it with the sword. It was second nature to him, as if he'd been born a swordsman, and the ball of crackling energy ricocheted harmlessly across the rooftop. Full of his new strength, Billy charged at the Magician, yelling at the top of his voice and sweeping the sword before him. The Runners gaped in wonder as they watched the Magician take a step back. He looked scared, and the children began their chanting again.

'BILLY, BILLY, BILLY!'

The Magician fought back with his ebony cane, but with a swipe of his sword Billy sliced a piece off his flapping black cloak. It blew away on the wind like a raggedy crow and the Magician seemed somehow frailer. Billy attacked again, and again the Magician fought back. The more confident Billy grew, the weaker the Magician became. He was on the verge of defeat, and in desperation he sent a jagged lightning bolt zipping towards Billy. It hit his sword, sending it flying from his hand, over the parapet wall and down to the ground below. Billy froze in horror.

'Ha! You fool!' the Magician exclaimed. 'Even with the sword you can't beat me. I AM INVINCIBLE. Now, go back to your cell, you pathetic upstart – all of you go back to your cells. The fun and games are over.'

But despite losing the legendary sword, Billy still felt full of confidence. He knew he had reached a moment of no return and that whatever happened next would decide his future. Was he going to be ruled by his fear for ever or was he going to stand up to it, sword or no sword?

'I'm not scared of you,' he shouted.

The whole of the crowd, Runners and night-children and creatures alike, held their breath as they wondered what would happen next. The silence seemed to go on for ages.

Then the Magician began to roar like the wind. His skin sparked with magic and he grew and grew until he towered over the crowd, his body spreading into a sheet of blackness filled with stars and spinning planets.

'I am the night,' boomed the Magician. 'You will all bow before me.'

The night-children began to scream, and his familiars quaked and shook as the folds of the Magician's cloak billowed and cracked and a hurricane whipped across the roof. It nearly lifted Billy off his feet, but he stood strong against the raging storm. Then the Magician was on him, his great expanse of darkness wrapping around him in a smothering embrace.

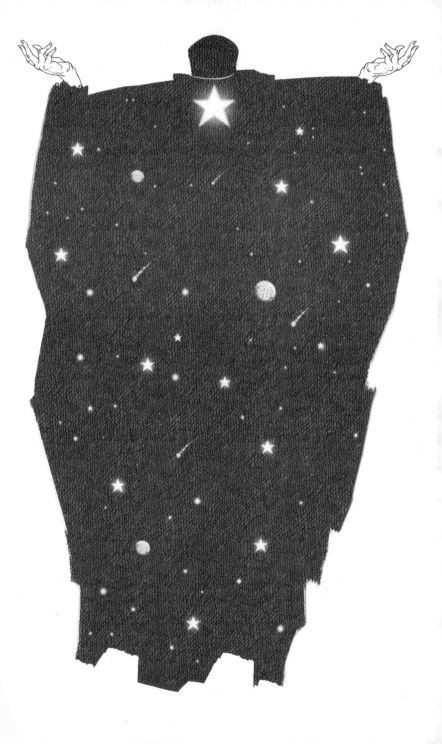

Billy gasped for breath. He felt he was being suffocated, but he was not going to give in. The clearest image of his dad formed in his mind.

Remember, Billy, no fear is too big to overcome, he had said, and Billy felt suddenly calm and in control.

'I AM NOT SCARED OF YOU ANY MORE,' he yelled.

The storm grew louder and wilder. It sounded as if the heavens might fall, but Billy stayed strong.

'I AM NOT SCARED.'

CRACK! There was an explosive bolt of lightning . . . and then silence. Total silence.

The storm had blown itself out, and the Magician was left standing in the middle of the vast roof, looking as weak as water and as withered as a rotten apple. His power was gone.

Billy turned to the crowd of Magician's familiars. They were trembling like jellies.

'I am not scared of you!' he yelled, and the crawlers, the creatures that haunted his worst nightmares, hissed and squealed and melted into a viscous pool that dribbled away down the drains.

Lightning stepped forward, emboldened by Billy.

'I'm not scared!' she cried – and her greatest

nightmare, the giant, thick-necked shadowmen, began to evaporate into thin air, bellowing like tortured bulls. The Magician looked on helplessly, and soon it was as if they'd never existed.

'We're not scared!' hollered the other Runners, joining in. Even the crowds of night-children who had lost all their memories of home, began to chant too, 'We're not scared; we're not scared.'

One by one all the children's fears vanished – the werehounds and collectors, the snufflers, witches and warlocks. Soon there were no nightmares left. Only the trembling Magician remained.

'WE'RE NOT SCARED!' roared the crowds of night-children.

'Aaargggh!' shrieked the Magician. It sounded like the cry of a lost soul, and he began to shrivel and squirm and got smaller . . . and smaller . . . and smaller. He shrank to the

size of a wriggling maggot and crackled and fizzed like a sparkler. Soon all that was left of him was a scorch mark on the ground.

Billy hurried over to where the Magician had been standing, worried there might be some vestige of him left, but he couldn't see anything. Not even a smut of ash.

'It's over!' he whispered to himself, and smiled.

21

The night-children swarmed around Billy. They looked shell-shocked, as if they couldn't quite believe what had happened. Billy felt dazed too. Then it hit him – *he had defeated the Magician!*

'Billy, I'm changing!' came a voice from the crowd, and Lightning stepped forward, holding her hand up for everyone to see. Her skin was flushing with its natural colour and her wide, staring eyes had shrunk to their normal size.

'And I remember my name!' she said, with a catch in her voice. 'I'm Abi!'

'My real name is Joe,' said Ace. He was changing back to his proper self too. 'I can remember where my house is!'

'I c-c-can remember everything,' cried Tom with a wide grin.

'You did it, Billy,' said Fleetfoot, stepping forward. 'I said you could.' Her wrinkled face became smooth as the years spent in the darkness drained away, leaving a bright young girl only recognizable by the sparkle in her eyes.

'Oh – look, everyone!' cried Tom, pointing to the night sky.

A great fiery globe was rising above the horizon and it flooded the sky with golden sunlight.

One by one, all the night-children were turning back to their proper form, and Billy recognized lots of children from his school. Others were strangers, some even wearing sweatshirts and trainers that looked years out of date.

I never knew so many children were scared of the dark, he thought.

Then, as the sun rose higher and the sky grew lighter, the fortress began to rumble beneath their feet.

'Uh-oh. I think it's time to go,' said Billy. 'Come on, let's get out of here!'

All the children, hundreds upon hundreds of them, ran for the doors and tumbled down the stairs. Jagged cracks snaked across the walls as they rushed through empty halls. Rubble began to fall from the ceilings and crashed all around them.

'Quick,' yelled Billy. 'The whole lot is coming down.' He dashed out of the Keep and into the lanes and courtyards. He saw the sword lying near a cloistered walkway and raced over to it.

'Leave it, Billy,' yelled Tom. 'It's too d-d-dangerous.' But there was no way Billy

was going to leave the back of his grandad's pocket watch behind. He crouched down, snapped it from the sword's blade and popped it back onto his watch. Then he ran, just as an archway collapsed and the mythical sword was buried beneath a tonne of falling rubble. He raced out of the main gate and into the streets of the town.

A mighty roar filled the air, and everyone turned to watch as the fortress towers toppled and the Magician's great Keep crumbled and collapsed. The ground shook as if it were the end of the world, and a choking pall of dust filled the air and spread through the town.

Coughing and spluttering, Billy peered through the cloud. There was nothing left of the fortress but a huge pile of rubble. He climbed onto a heap of debris and faced the crowd of children.

'It's time to go home,' he shouted.

'How?' asked a voice in the crowd. 'Where do we go?'

'Can you remember the place where you first arrived here?'

'Yeah, over by the bakery,' said Joe.

'I ended up here when I went under the canal bridge,' said Abi.

Everyone began to remember, and they all started talking at the same time.

'Then go back there, wherever it is,' shouted Billy above the hubbub. 'Retrace your steps and I'm sure you will get home.'

The children immediately scattered, running off to different parts of town, whooping with joy. Abi went up to Billy and planted a

smacker of a kiss on his cheek.

'Bye, Billy, and thanks for everything,' she said, a look of concern shadowing her face. 'But what happens when we do get home? I've been away for ages. Fleetfoot's been imprisoned here for years. Will our mums or dads or whatever be old – will they even remember who we are? And will we even be going back to the same time?'

'Sorry, I just don't know,' said Billy. It was something that had been bothering him too. 'Anywhere's got to be better than this cursed place, though, hasn't it?'

'Yeah, I just wish we could all go home together, you know,' she said with a smile. 'Be friends in real life too.'

Then she and Ace, who was really Joe, and Dusty, who was really Freddie, and Grubby who really *was* Grubby, all said their goodbyes.

'What about you, Tom?' asked Billy, when they had gone and the two friends were left on their own.

'I ended up here when I followed that cat, near the park,' said Tom. 'I'd best go back that w-w-way.'

'See you soon,' said Billy, and the two friends parted, Tom going one way and Billy heading back to Merlin Place. *I hope this works*, he said to himself.

The streets were still eerily empty, but rays of sunshine were starting to break through the pall of dust that enveloped the town.

Billy ran up the street to his house and

cautiously tried the front door. His key turned in the lock, and he stepped inside. But it still seemed deserted, and there were even a few jackdaw feathers lying about. His heart sank. Nothing had changed.

He looked out of the bay window. It was a bright, sunny day, but the street remained empty and silent, and tears began to blur his vision – but then a car zoomed along the road, and a couple pushed a baby's buggy past the end of the drive. Billy rushed out of the front door, down the drive and onto his bustling street. Everything seemed back to normal – but was it? Where was his mum?

Full of foreboding, Billy ran back inside the house. Now, a delicious smell of baking wafted from the kitchen, and when he cautiously opened the door a crack, he saw his mum busy preparing tea, as if nothing had happened. A feeling of joyous relief swept through him like a huge wave.

Billy checked his pocket watch. It was ticking away merrily, and read half-past five – but half-past five on what day? How was he going to explain to his mum and dad where he'd been for all this time?

He barged noisily into the kitchen and his mum looked up from her work with a stern look on her face.

'You're late,' she said. 'I was starting to worry. Where on earth . . . ?' but her sentence was cut short as Billy ran over and gave her a huge hug. He was so pleased to be home.

'What day is it, Mum?' he asked, a little nervously.

'Friday, of course, silly!'

So, no time had passed at all for people at home – it must be like that for all the other night-children, and Billy felt certain they were all home safely. Wherever, or whenever, that was.

'Sorry, Mum,' he said. 'I lost all track of time.'

Billy's mum was so surprised by this show of affection her tetchy mood vanished. 'Never mind. No harm done,' she said, giving him a peck on his forehead.

Billy went upstairs to his bedroom, collapsed on his bed and thought about everything that had happened. He knew the sun would set that night and darkness flood the world, and he knew branches might tap against his window and the dark echo to strange noises, but he wasn't worried any more. He had stood up to the Magician, and he had won.

And tomorrow, he would go to Tom's for his friend's birthday, and he would stay overnight.

Billy took the watch from his pocket and studied it. His dad had been right. Grandad's watch *was* a talisman, and it had protected him through the horrifying twists and turns of the Night's Realm. He wiped a smear of dirt from the engraving of the sword on its case, and put the watch safely under his pillow. Then Billy went downstairs for his tea.

Did you think this was over? Well, you are mistaken. Somewhere in your big bright world there are children still petrified of the night. Scared enough to send a small scrap from my shredded cloak flapping into the air like a dark moth. Scared enough for it to grow and shift in shape until, with an exultant scream, I AM BACK.

Now, as I look out over my ruined kingdom, a skulking crawler has returned to sit at my side like an obedient dog. I will have to start building all over again, and you are most welcome to come and help me – but first I must deal with Billy Jones...